"How'd you lose your hearing?"

He nearly dropped. "How…?" He stared into her wide, clear green eyes, sucked in a breath and accepted that the secret was out. "Explosion, about thirteen months ago."

She shifted the baby on her hip. "About the same time CJ was born, then."

What a coincidence, he thought, looking at the baby. She'd been gaining something precious while he was losing his hearing, along with life as he'd known it, his career, the future he'd envisioned for himself.

ARLENE JAMES,

the author of over forty novels, now resides outside of Dallas, Texas, with her husband. Arlene says, "The rewards of motherhood have indeed been extraordinary for me. Yet I've looked forward to this new stage of my life." Her need to write is greater than ever, a fact that frankly amazes her as she's been at it since the eighth grade! Arlene reflects, "Camp meetings, mission work and the church where my parents and grandparents were prominent members permeate my Oklahoma childhood memories. It was a golden time, which sustains me yet. However, only as a young, widowed mother did I truly begin growing in my personal relationship with the Lord. Through adversity, He blessed me in countless ways, one of which is a second marriage so loving and romantic it still feels like courtship!"

THE HEART'S VOICE

VOICE

ARLENE JAMES

Love Inspired.

Published by Steeple Hill Books™

STEEPLE HILL BOOKS

Steeple
Hill®

ISBN 0-373-87271-2

THE HEART'S VOICE

www.SteepleHill.com

Printed in U.S.A.

So that you incline your ear to wisdom,
and apply your heart to understanding.

—Proverbs 2:2

Chapter One

"Here's your chance."

Becca looked up from the shelf of canned goods she was stocking, glanced at her mother-in-law, Abby Kinder, and immediately turned her attention to the row of shopping carts parked along the front wall of the Kinder grocery store. Daniel Holden, tall and straight, tugged a cart free and aimed it toward the produce section. Becca felt a flutter of excitement inside her chest. With Easter just a week away, the time was right to begin repairs on her dilapidated ranch house. The weather was fine, she had managed to save a sum of money and it seemed that God had finally provided someone to do the work, at least according to the town scuttlebutt.

"You just don't expect the Marine Corps to turn out expert carpenters," she commented quietly. "I mean, soldiers, of course, and maybe mechanics, computer techs, even desk clerks, but 'carpenter' just doesn't seem to fit the mold.''

Abby chuckled, swiping a feather duster over boxes of pasta dinners. ''You'd be amazed at the kind of training the military offers. Cody considered signing up, you know.'' She smiled wistfully, the pain of loss clouding her clear gray eyes even after these many months, but then she shook her silver head, the bun at the nape of her neck sliding from side to side, and her customary cheer reasserted itself. ''His dad and I thought it was too dangerous, so then he goes out and takes up rodeo.'' She waved the feather duster, as if to say no one could predict what life would hold. Becca knew exactly what she meant. After years on the rodeo circuit, Cody had been killed in his own backyard by a high-strung stud horse.

Becca squeezed her mother-in-law's hand and went back to emptying the box on the tiered flatbed cart at her side, giving Dan Holden time to finish his shopping. Resolutely putting thoughts of her late husband out of her mind, she concentrated on the proposition she meant to make the tall ex-marine with the carpenter's skill.

Every day she drove past the Holden house on her way to and from work. Empty for longer than she'd lived in the sleepy little town of Rain Dance, Oklahoma, the elegant place had gradually taken on an air of abandonment and decay, but over the past three or four months that Dan had lived there, the old-fashioned two-story prairie cottage had seemed to come alive and take back its dignity. Now it stood fit and neat, as straight and tall as its owner and occupant, who just might be the answer to Becca's prayers.

When Dan turned his shopping cart toward the single checkout stand, Becca quickly wiped her hands on her apron and moved behind the counter. As Dan placed the first items on the rubber mat, Becca gave him a bright smile.

"How're you keeping, Mr. Holden?"

He nodded, but made no reply. She'd noticed that he was a quiet man, rarely speaking and often seeming shy, though with his looks she couldn't imagine why. He'd pretty much kept to himself since returning to Rain Dance after an absence of some ten or twelve years, but Becca figured he'd just been busy with the house. She rang up the first items and bagged them, talking as she worked.

"The word around town is that you're something of a carpenter."

He made no comment, didn't so much as look at her as he placed several cans on the counter. Becca licked her lips and took the plunge.

"Fact is, I'm looking for someone to help me fix up my old house, Mr. Holden, and I was wondering if you might be interested in taking on the project?"

It seemed a good idea. To her knowledge he didn't have a job, not that there were many to be had in this part of south central Oklahoma. Most folks depended on ranching, farming and intermittent oil field work to keep afloat, or else they were pensioners making the most of their retirement income. Living was cheap, if limited, in Rain Dance, which boasted a population of some 500 residents within the narrow confines of its city limits and perhaps an equal number in the surrounding area.

Without ever making eye contact, Dan Holden placed a carton of milk on the counter and reached back into his shopping cart for a box of cereal. She took his lack of reply as a good sign. At least he hadn't refused her outright.

"I've got a little money put aside," she told him, "and you've done such a fine job on your place, I was thinking we could maybe help each other out."

He plunked down a jar of pickles and a squirt bottle of mustard. She reached for the mustard, judging it a perfect fit for the space left in the shopping bag that she was packing. Their hands collided, and he looked up with a jerk, as if she'd burned him. She tried that smile again.

"So what do you think?"

He frowned as if puzzled, then muttered, "I think I have everything I need."

Becca felt her smile wilt. "I see." Tamping down her disappointment, she quickly rang up the rest of his purchase. "I guess that means you're not interested in the job?" He didn't dignify that with a reply, so she gulped and asked, "Might you be able to recommend someone from around here who could help me?'' She'd been asking that question of everyone in town, and his name was the only one that ever seemed to come up.

Dan peered at the digital readout provided by the cash register and plucked bills from his wallet. She counted out his change, figuring that he was thinking over his answer, and left it on the counter. He picked it up, coin by coin, gathered his three bags of groceries and walked out.

Becca's jaw dropped, but she quickly snapped her mouth shut again. The man hadn't answered her with so much as a shrug.

Abby had been hovering nearby with her feather duster, listening unabashedly to every word. She now looked at Becca with sad confusion on her face. ''Well, he's sure changed. The Dan Holden I remember was a polite, outgoing young man. He wasn't much more than a boy, but still, that's not the same Dan Holden who left here for college. That's all I've got to say.''

''I wonder what changed him,'' Becca mused, leaning a hip against the counter.

''God knows,'' Abby replied. ''God always knows, and that's what matters, honey. If Dan can't or won't help you, God'll send someone else. You'll see.''

Becca smiled and put aside her disappointment, knowing that her mother-in-law was right. She wouldn't have been so certain a few years ago, but she had learned, thanks to the Kinders. When she'd first arrived in Oklahoma as a nineteen-year-old bride of only days, she'd thought she'd made a terrible mistake. She'd met Cody at a rodeo and married the cute cowboy after knowing him for only two weeks. The rodeo life had seemed exciting to a country girl reared on an Iowa farm, but then she'd realize that she'd be spending most of her time in Rain Dance, which had seemed precisely the sort of place from which she'd thought she'd escaped, a dying town peopled with old folks and country yokels.

Then Abby and John Odem Kinder had opened their hearts and their lives to her. They'd shared their small house, their affection and, most important, their faith, and almost before she'd realized what was happening Rain Dance had become home—and she had become a mother to a blond, blue-eyed baby girl. Cody had eventually scraped together enough winnings to buy them a place of their own on a quarter section three and half miles northeast of town.

The house had needed work even then, but the ranch had needed a good pair of breeding stock even more. They were hoping to start the horse herd that would provide the income that would keep Cody at home with his growing family, as Becca was pregnant again. Even without the much-needed repairs on the house, she wouldn't think of living anywhere else now, not even after finding herself a young widow with two children to support.

Rain Dance had its limitations, but she knew in her heart that this was where the good Lord meant her to be, so this was where she'd stay—even if she could see daylight through some walls of her little house.

Becca shepherded her daughter, Jemmy, into the pew near the front of the church where the Kinders sat, smiling as the four-year-old moppet preened in the simple blue-and-white-polka-dotted dress sewn for her by her grandmother. With her pale blond hair twisted into curls that most likely wouldn't last the service and a white straw hat tied with a blue ribbon under her chubby chin, she had sat for photos on the front steps of the narrow orange-brick church, giggling as John Odem had snapped away with his camera. Thirteen-month-old CJ had gone up onto his knees, trying to filch plastic eggs from his sister's Easter basket, his shirttail poking out of his navy blue shorts, matching bow tie seriously askew.

Finally Abby had brought the picture taking to a halt, warning that they would be late if they delayed any longer. Eager to show off her finery, Jemmy had insisted on accompanying her mother to the nursery, where CJ could play without disturbing the service, while her grandparents secured seats in the crowded sanctuary. By the time the middle-aged nursery attendant had finished gushing over how

Jem's dress matched her blue eyes, the pianist had started to play the opening prelude.

As mother and daughter slipped into the pew, Becca smiled at the family in the seats behind them and patiently lifted her gaze toward the rear of the church while Jemmy climbed up onto the cushioned seat. Dan Holden stood in the doorway, a look of consternation on his face. Becca was struck by how handsome he was, standing there with his military bearing in well-pressed slacks, shirt and tie, his square jaw cleanly shaven, short, light brown hair neatly combed, sky-blue eyes searching the crowded pews for a seat.

She'd seen him here before, of course, but he usually slipped in a little late and took a seat on the aisle in the very last pew and then was gone again before she and her family had worked their way to the door. Today, however, even the back pews were packed. She saw him hesitate and then turn slightly as if to leave. Something in her couldn't let that happen. It was Easter Sunday, the day of all days when a Christian should be in church. Beckoning him with a slight crook of her hand, she quickly turned and slid into the pew, crowding close to her daughter in order to leave space for him on the aisle.

For several long seconds she didn't know whether or not he would take her up on her invitation, but then she felt his silent presence at her side and glanced up with a welcoming smile. Color stood in small, bright red patches high on his cheek-bones, but he nodded thanks and folded his long frame onto the bench seat, elbows pulled tight to his sides. The pastor already stood in the pulpit, and he immediately lifted his voice to welcome all to God's house and comment on how nice it was to see so many in the congregation.

A few minutes later the music leader took over and got them all onto their feet for the first hymn of the morning. Becca joined in the singing. Jemmy climbed up into her grandfather's arms so she could see better, while Abby held a hymnal for him. His gravelly bass voice boomed so loudly that Jemmy covered her ears with her hands, which was exactly what John Odem had intended. It was a game they played, one of many. John liked to say that one of the most important lessons he'd learned in his nearly seventy years was to have as much fun as possible to help balance the difficulty that life often dealt. Having fun definitely included teasing his granddaughter. Smiling indulgently, Becca glanced at Dan Holden out of the corner of her eye. To her surprise Dan stared straight ahead, rigid and silent.

Realizing that he didn't have a hymnal, Becca briefly considered offering to share her own, but his stiffness made her uncertain. Compelled to seek an-other remedy, she looked down the pew, spying an extra hymnal in the pew pocket in front of her mother-in-law. Becca caught Abby's eye and pointed to the hymnal. Abby plucked it up and passed it to her. Becca immediately handed her own hymnal to Dan Holden, opened to the correct page.

He jerked, as if shocked by the gesture, and shook his head. His hand dipped with the weight of the heavy book before his gaze locked on her face, blue eyes piercing hers. Something there made Becca's breath catch, something intense and aching. His gaze moved from her face to the music on the page. The next instant he snapped the book shut, dropped it into the pew pocket in front of him and clasped his hands behind his back, a proud soldier at ease before a commanding officer.

Stung, Becca ducked her chin, brow beetled as she tried to figure out this guy. What was his problem, anyway? One moment he seemed charmingly shy and the next downright rude. It was almost as if he didn't know how to act around people. She now wanted to ignore him, but since he occupied the space right next to her, she couldn't help being uncomfortably aware of his every movement, or lack of it, to be more precise. During the sermon she noticed that he never took his eyes off the pastor's face. He appeared rapt, almost eerily so, and he seemed genuinely moved at several points. By the time the service progressed to the invitation, her puzzlement had deepened significantly. Dan Holden's actions and reactions just didn't seem to add up, and Becca's curiosity had definitely been piqued by the time the service ended.

As expected, the instant they were dismissed, he

turned into the aisle, but Becca impulsively reached out to trap him with a hand clamped firmly upon his forearm. He turned wary eyes of such intense attention on her that she once more caught her breath, but the next moment she heard herself babbling, "Oh, Mr. Holden, you remember me, don't you? I'm Becca Kinder."

"From the store," he mumbled in a voice so low that she had to lean close to hear him.

"That's right."

He glanced past her, his blue gaze sliding over Jemmy to John Odem. Becca released him, a little abashed by her forwardness now. He nodded at John and said, a little too loudly this time, "Mr. Kinder."

"Hello, Dan."

But Holden's gaze had slid right on past John Odem to Abby. "Ma'am," he said, and then he slipped away, edging and elbowing his way through the throng moving sluggishly toward the door. By the time Becca gathered her daughter to her side, he was gone.

"That man is downright peculiar," she said to no one in particular.

"Aw, I bet he's just having a little trouble settling into civilian life," John Odem said, tweaking Jemmy's ear.

Becca ducked her head. "I'm sure you're right."

"Maybe you ought to call on him, John," Abby suggested, crowding her family out into the aisle.

"Sure thing," John Odem agreed. "I'll go soon as that side of beef is delivered in the morning. Then you can do the butchering."

"Oh, no, you don't," Abby retorted.

"Why not?" John Odem asked innocently. "I figure it's time for some thumb soup."

"What's thumb soup?" Jemmy wanted to know.

"That's what we'll be having for supper once Grandma lops off her thumb with my butcher knife."

"Ewwww!" Jemmy exclaimed, wrinkling her nose.

"Stop that, John Odem Kinder," Abby scolded with mock severity. "We'll be having no disgusting soups, sugar," she assured her granddaughter, "because I'm not doing any butchering."

"You two are going to put this child off her feed for a month," Becca said reprovingly. "Honey, no one makes soup out of thumbs. Grandpa's just joshing you."

"Grandpa!" Jemmy scolded, sounding for all the world just like her grandmother.

John Odem laughed delightedly. When they drew even with the pastor, however, he did ask about Dan Holden.

"Anybody talk to that Holden boy since he came home, Pastor?"

The middle-aged preacher shook his head. "Not for lack of trying, John. He doesn't seem to have a phone. Shep Marcum and I have stopped by the house a few times, but no one ever came to the door. He seems to be keeping pretty busy.''

"He seems to be keeping to himself," Abby commented, and the pastor nodded.

"That, too.''

Becca bit her lip, mulling over this information. It seemed that Dan Holden didn't want to have anything do with anyone around Rain Dance, but if that were so, then why had he come back here?

The puzzle of Dan Holden just wouldn't leave Becca alone. She lay in her bed that night trying to decide what it was she'd seen in his eyes that disturbed her so, but try as she might, she couldn't come up with a solid explanation. Her first guess was loneliness, but why would a lonely man hold everyone at bay, avoiding conversation? Did his past hide something dark that he feared others would discover, something that shamed him? Maybe it was something that had forced him out of the Marine Corps, but what?

Maybe he was AWOL, absent from the military without leave.

No, that didn't make any sense. He would be plenty easy to find in a little town like Rain Dance, especially since he had family connections to the community. Besides, a Christian man with a guilty conscience would be compelled to make things right, and she felt in her heart of hearts that Dan was a true Christian. She'd seen the tears standing in his eyes when the pastor had described the suffering of Christ as He'd willingly paid the sin debt for all of humanity, witnessed the quiet intensity of his emotion as he'd listened to the dramatic reading of Scripture, watched his silent joy as the Resurrection was proclaimed. Yes, Dan believed. It was obvious. So why, then, did he bolt like a scalded hound whenever anyone tried to connect with him?

Maybe it was just her. Maybe she was the one he didn't want to have anything to do with, and he really had been busy when the others had come to call. It was a lowering thought, and one she felt compelled to put to the test on Tuesday next.

She stayed late to close the store on Tuesdays and Thursdays, so John Odem and Abby could have their dinner together at a decent hour, and it had become the family custom for the kids to eat with their grandparents and on occasion stay overnight. This was just such an occasion, so Becca found herself driving alone about eight-thirty in the evening past the Holden place on her way out of town. As she drew close to the house, she naturally glanced toward it.

Dan Holden's profile appeared in an open living-room window. He was sitting in a big, comfy chair watching a large television screen. The way he sat there, so very still, hands resting on the wide rolled arms of the chair, had a lonely feel about it, and something inside Becca said, "Stop."

She shivered, as if God Himself had tapped her on the shoulder, and before she could even think to do it, her foot had moved from the gas pedal to the brake. She sat there for a moment, the engine of her battered old car rumbling in competition with a cricket calling for his mate. Then with a sigh she yielded to her initial impulse and turned the vehicle into Dan Holden's drive. She parked and got out, leaving the keys in the ignition as usual. Reluctantly she let her tired feet take her along the hedged walkway to the front steps and then up those steps to the broad, sheltered porch. From this angle, the light of the TV flickered against the windowpane, but now only that persistent cricket could be heard.

Becca knocked on the door. She thought its berry-red paint made a very pretty display with the pristine white of the siding, new grass-green roof and black shutters. She waited, but the contrary man couldn't be bothered to answer his door.

She tried again, her irritation growing. No response. Well, that took the proverbial cake. The man obviously didn't want or need a friend. It must have been a perverse imp who had compelled her to stop, but this time she was going to let Dan Holden know that his rudeness had been noted and marked. In a rare fit of pique she moved to stand directly in front of the window, which she pecked insistently with the tip of one forefinger before turning to stomp across the porch and down the steps on her way back to her car. Her feet had barely hit the paved walk when that red door finally opened.

"Who's there?"

For an instant she considered giving him a dose of his own medicine, just stomping off into the night without another word, but that was not Becca's way.

"It's me," she said, somewhat grudgingly. "Becca Kinder. I was just—"

The porch light suddenly blazed. "Mrs. Kinder," he said, surprise evident in his voice. "Is that you?"

Becca frowned. "I just told you so, didn't I?"

"Come up here into the light," he dictated, stepping out onto the porch, "and tell me what I can do for you." His voice had a stilted, uneven quality to it, as if he wasn't quite sure what tone to use.

Sorry that she'd come at all, Becca climbed the trio of steps again, realizing that she had no idea what she'd meant to say to him in the first place. An honest response was always the best one, so she licked her lips and said, "I was hoping you might be interested in working on my house now."

He cocked his head, as if he found something odd about that. "Sorry. Not possible."

"But you've done such fine work on this place," Becca heard herself arguing.

"Thank you," he said with a small smile. "Now I'm doing the garage apartment out back. Might rent it out."

Becca nodded, disappointed all over again. At least he had an excuse to offer this time. That was progress. Of a sort. "I see. Well, if that doesn't pan out and you find yourself needing work…"

He shook his head. "I'm keeping busy."

That was something with which she could certainly identify. "Just not enough hours in the day, are there?"

"Suppose not."

She searched for something else to say and finally gestured toward the western end of the south-facing house. "You ought to hang a swing over there."

He glanced at the end of the porch and back again. "Think so?"

"And paint it red," she added.

He rubbed his chin, smiling so brightly that she felt a kick in her chest. "Just might do that."

She felt positively warm all of a sudden, and the thought occurred to her that he was a downright likable man when he wasn't being standoffish. "You know what else would be pretty?" she asked, basking in that male smile. He shook his head. "Two big white pots right here on either side of the steps, just spilling over with flowers, geraniums maybe, red to match the swing."

"My grandma used to keep flowerpots there."

"Well, there you go," Becca said.

He nodded. "I'll look into it sometime."

"Maybe when you're finished with that garage apartment."

"Maybe," he said, making it sound like two words instead of one.

Completely out of topics for discussion now, Becca glanced at the window looking into his living room. "You're missing your program," she finally offered lamely, "and morning comes early for me, so I'd best be going."

"Good night."

"Good night, Mr. Holden." She turned to go, but then a fresh thought hit her. "You know, there's a Bible study on Wednesday evenings that you might want—" She broke off. He'd already retreated and was closing the door. She brought her hands to her hips. There he went again! The man had practically locked up while she was still talking.

From the corner of her eye she caught sight of him moving back into the living room and reclaiming his seat in the chair. Must be some mighty interesting TV program he was watching. Curious, she stepped to one side and looked at the set. A commercial was playing, but she did note one interesting thing. The television seemed to be displaying closed captions, the words spelling out across the bottom of the screen. She was too far away to read them, and it could have been a disclaimer of some sort for the commercial, but she left wondering if she might not have discovered the clue to Dan Holden's odd behavior.

Chapter Two

Dan came into the store on Friday morning, a half day for Becca. He smiled and waved as he pulled his cart from the queue, then purchased milk and eggs and a piece of salt pork for "a mess of beans," as he said at the checkout.

"You must be missing military chow," she teased.

"Must be," he agreed shyly.

He turned his attention to a rack of television program guides mounted near the checkout, and Becca deliberately asked, "What sort are you having?"

He made no reply, just as she had expected, so she repeated the question once she had his attention again.

"Navy beans," he said with a grin. "Called them something else in the Corps."

"I prefer good old reds myself."

He chuckled. "Red seems to be a theme with you."

"I like red," she admitted. "That'll be $9.17."

"Bet it's a good color on you," he said, and then ducked his head as that very shade bloomed on the ridges of his cheeks. He dug out a ten-dollar bill and plunked it on the table, mumbling, "You have a good day now."

"Oh, I will," she said, purposely not looking at him as she extracted his change from the cash drawer. "I'm expecting John Travolta to pick me up for lunch in his private jet." She peeked at him to see how he'd taken that, or if he'd even heard it, but he was already making for the door with his groceries. "Hey!" she called out. "Your change!" She wasn't the least surprised when he just kept on walking.

"What's the matter, honey?" Abby asked, appearing from the little office blocked off across the aisle from the checkout.

Becca dropped the coins into her apron pocket. "Dan Holden just forgot his change, that's all."

"How much?"

"Eighty-three cents."

"Oh, well, just give it to him next time he comes in."

"I'll take care of it," Becca said with a smile.

Abby nodded and turned back into the office, where she was tabulating invoices for payment.

Becca patted the small bulge in her pocket and decided that she was going to pay another call on the handsome ex-marine, and this time they were going to have an honest talk.

Dan saw the flashing light on the panel mounted on the kitchen wall. Connected to a motion detector, it signaled him whenever someone approached his front door. He'd installed the panels in his bedroom, bath and here in the kitchen, and eventually he meant to have them in every room. Originally he'd thought he wouldn't need one in the living room, as it overlooked the porch, but little Becca Kinder's visit a few nights earlier had shown him that he wasn't as observant as he'd judged himself to be. He wondered how many other visitors he'd missed because he'd been too proud to admit that he might overlook what he couldn't hear.

Rising from the chair, he left his sandwich on the table and walked down the central hall past the staircase to the front door. Upon opening the door, he didn't know who was more surprised, Becca Kinder, who had apparently not yet knocked, or him at seeing pretty little Becca on his doorstep again, this time with a fat baby perched on one hip. It looked to be a boy.

"Hi."

"Hi, yourself," she said, holding out her right hand.

"What's this?" he asked, putting out his own palm.

"The change you forgot at the store this morning."

"Oh!"

He felt the burn of embarrassment again, and it galled him. What was it about this girl that kept him blushing like some awkward preteen? He slipped the coins into the front pocket of his jeans. Catching movement from the corner of his eye, he glanced left and spied her little girl skipping merrily across his porch, pale hair flopping. Becca was not a girl, but a woman and a mother, he reminded himself, and he'd do well to remember it. He still thought of Cody Kinder as the happy-go-lucky kid he'd once known, clomping around in a droopy cowboy hat and boots two sizes too large. Now here stood his family.

"Didn't have to bring this," he said, looking her in the eye. He always worried that he wouldn't get his volume right, but she neither winced nor leaned in closer.

She shrugged, and he dropped his gaze to her mouth. It was a pretty little mouth, a perfect pink bow. "No problem. It's on my way home. Besides, I wanted to ask you something."

He assumed that it had to do with her house and the repairs she seemed to think she needed. "All right."

"How'd you lose your hearing?"

He nearly dropped from shock. "How..." He stared into her wide, clear green eyes, sucked in a breath and accepted that the secret was out. "Explosion."

She nodded matter-of-factly, no trace of pity in her expression. She was a pretty thing, with her fine, straight, light golden-blond hair cropped bluntly just above her shoulders, the bangs wisping randomly across her forehead. Those soft olive-green eyes were big and round, but not too large for her wide oval face with its pointed chin and small, tip-tilted nose. Completely devoid of cosmetics, her golden skin literally glowed, and her dusty-pink mouth truly intrigued him. She was so easy to lip-read.

"I figured it was something like that," she said. "Mind if I ask how long ago it was?"

He shook his head, as much to clear it as in answer to her question. "About thirteen months."

She shifted the baby on her hip. "About the same time CJ was born, then."

What a coincidence, he thought, looking at the baby. She'd been gaining something precious while he was losing his hearing, along with life as he'd known it, his career, the future he'd envisioned for himself. Keeping his expression carefully bland, he switched his gaze back to her face.

"How did you know?"

"Little things. Abby says you were always friendly and outgoing before." He winced at the implication. "But you don't reply sometimes when you're spoken to." She grinned. "I thought you were rude."

He closed his eyes, appalled that he wasn't as smart as he'd assumed, then he opened them again to find that she was still speaking.

"...weren't singing and the way you watched the pastor so intently when he was preaching. Then there were the closed captions on the TV the other night."

He waved a hand, feeling ridiculous. Had he really believed that he could fool everyone? He'd thought that if he kept to himself and was careful he could lead something close to a normal life. Now he knew that wasn't true, and he felt sick in a way that he hadn't since he'd realized that he was never going to hear another sound. For some reason he felt compelled to try to explain it to her.

"It's not obvious at first."

"No, it's not. Took me a while to figure it out."

"I'm not comfortable announcing it." He hoped he hadn't stumbled over the word *comfortable*.

"I understand. And why should you if you don't have to? How did you learn to read lips so well, by the way?"

"Training."

"Guess that's one good thing about the military, huh? They take care of their own."

"That's right. Helps that I wasn't born this way."

"I see. Is your deafness why you won't work on my house?" she asked.

He rubbed a hand over his face. "Yes."

She bit her lip. "Okay. Well, you don't have to worry that I'll say anything to anybody. I mean, if that's the way you want it."

He forced a smile. "Thank you."

"But since I already know about your problem, there's really no reason why you can't help me out, is there?"

He opened his mouth, then closed it again. She had a point. He sighed, then hoped she hadn't heard. It was hard to tell with her. "You better come in."

She shook her head, glancing at her daughter, who continued skipping. The child appeared to be singing to herself. Becca hefted the boy to a more comfortable position, and he noticed how small and childlike her hands were before quickly jerking his gaze back to her face. "That's okay. Jenny likes playing on your porch."

He wasn't sure about the name. "Jenny?"

"No. J-e-m-m-y. Jemmy."

"Jemmy." He pointed at the boy. "CJ?"

"For Cody John, after his daddy and his grandpa."

Dan nodded his understanding. The child was huge, with fat cheeks and thighs, or his mother was very small, or both. Either way, she looked much too young to have two children.

"So will you help me fix up my house?"

She might be young, but she was persistent. Dan rubbed a hand over the nape of his neck. Was this God's will, that he work on her house? He was having a hard time figuring out what God had in store for him these days. He'd come home to Rain Dance simply because he had to go somewhere after the Marine Corps had medically retired him, and at thirty he didn't like feeling dependent on his parents, especially with his sister, Gayla, busily planning her fall wedding. By helping out Becca Kinder he'd at least be keeping busy.

"No promises," he finally said, "but I'll take a look."

She literally bounced, as excited as if she'd just won the lottery. "Oh, thank you, Mr. Holden!"

"Dan," he corrected automatically.

She smiled. "And I'm Becca."

"Becca," he repeated carefully. "Not Becky?"

"Not Becky," she confirmed, "but short for Rebecca."

"Okay, Becca. When and where?"

She started to answer him, but then she suddenly turned away. He followed her gaze and saw that Jemmy was about to slip off the end of the porch and down between the hedges. She stopped and cast a measuring glance at her mother, then resumed skipping again. Becca smiled at him and said, "As far as how to find us, just head east straight on out of town to the second section line. Then turn back north. We're on the left just over a mile down.''

He smiled because she hadn't altered the speed or manner in which she normally spoke. ''Two miles east. One north. On the left.''

''Right. There's no section line road there, but you'll see the name on the mailbox.''

''Kinder,'' he surmised.

''That's it.'' She flapped a hand happily. ''Oh, you don't know how long I've waited for this! See you then.'' As she turned to go, he realized that he'd missed something important, and without even thinking, he reached out and snagged her wrist. A jolt of heat lanced up his arm. He instantly released her.

''Sorry. Uh, when?''

Her eyes grew even rounder, and apology was suddenly written all over her face. ''I turned my head. Jemmy was about to crawl off into the bushes, and I didn't even think.''

''It's all right.'' He brought his hands to his hips, just to be sure he didn't accidentally reach out for her again. ''Tell me when.''

''Monday's my day off, so anytime Monday would be great for me.''

He nodded. ''Monday.''

She smiled, and he drew back, that smile doing strange things to his insides. He wondered if her husband was going to be there, and hoped that he was. It would be best to deal with Cody. Perhaps he should suggest it, but she was already turning away again, calling the girl to her side as she went. Dan backed up and closed the door. Then he suddenly remembered something he'd seen.

She wore her wedding ring on her right hand and no ring at all on her left. Thinking quickly, he weighed the significance of that, and then he remembered something else. One day down at the store he'd seen two women standing in front of the deli case, watching John Odem carve up a ham. One had leaned close to the other and apparently whispered something that had stuck with him. *What a shame about the boy.*

He knew now what it meant. Cody Kinder had died. That explained why Dan hadn't seen him around at all since his return, even why Becca had come to ask for his help. He thought of the boy he had known and felt a keen sense of loss tinged with shame. Cody had been younger than him, so they hadn't been buddies or anything, but Dan had always liked the kid as well as his parents, who had fairly doted on their only child. And to think that all this time he'd been too busy feeling his own loss to even realize what they had suffered.

He sighed and bowed his head.

Okay. I get it. Lots of folks have lost lots more than me. The least I can do is help Becca Kinder with whatever repairs she's needing. And I'll try to be less prideful from now on, Lord. Really I will.

For the first time in a long while a real sense of

purpose filled him, and it felt good. Really good. He went back to his lunch, walking down the hall to the kitchen, completely ignorant of a loud squeak at a certain spot in the clean, highly polished hardwood floor.

Becca couldn't say why she looked for him to come into the store on Saturday, but she was disappointed when it didn't happen. Ever since he'd admitted his deafness to her, she'd felt that they shared a bond along with the secret. And yet she felt torn about the secret itself. Whatever his reasons for not publicly acknowledging his lack of hearing, it served only to keep him isolated. Most people would gladly accommodate his condition, allowing him to get back into the swing of things around the community. Perhaps with him working around her house—and she couldn't imagine that he wouldn't be—God would give her the words to say to convince him to let people know about his disadvantage.

She didn't see any reason to wait for Monday to speak to him, however, so on Sunday she kept an eye out, and sure enough he slipped in late and took up his customary spot on the back row. She didn't signal to him to come up front, though there was space in the pew, but she did rush out at the first possible moment, leaving Jemmy in the care of the Kinders. With barely a nod for the pastor, she hurried through the narrow foyer and down the front steps, catching up with him beneath a big beech tree that grew near the sidewalk and overhung the dusty parking area.

He stopped and turned when she tapped him on the shoulder. She suddenly found herself smiling like a goose.

"What's your hurry?"

He glanced down at the key in his hand and said softly, "Bean casserole."

She waited until he looked up at her again before she said, "Guess there's no point in inviting you to Sunday dinner, then, huh?" She'd meant to tease but realized belatedly that she was serious. At any rate, he missed the inflection.

"Nice of you." He shook his head apologetically. "Not a good idea."

"Because you'd be uncomfortable around John Odem and Abby," she surmised.

He seemed a little surprised by that, but then he didn't have any way of knowing that she routinely took Sunday dinner with the Kinders. "Yes," he said, and she had the distinct feeling that it wasn't exactly the truth—not all of it, anyway.

Suddenly struck by how forward she was being, she looked away. That's when Shep Marcum stopped by to shake Dan's hand and invite him to the men's Sunday-school class.

"Thank you for mentioning it, Mr. Marcum," Dan said slowly and politely, but just a tad too loud. Then again, Shep was nearly John Odem's age and hard of hearing. Maybe he wouldn't notice. "I'll think on it."

"You do that, son," Shep said, clapping Dan on the shoulder. "We'd sure be glad to have you." He glanced at Becca and winked. "Looking mighty pretty again today, Becca. That's a right attractive dress you're wearing."

Becca grinned. "Shep, it's the same dress I wear every other Sunday, and you know it."

"Well, it's still a nice one," he said jauntily, stepping off the sidewalk.

She laughed and slid a wry look at Dan. "He says that about the other one, too."

"The other one?"

"My other Sunday dress."

"Ah."

He looked down at his feet, missing the greeting called out by the Platters—not that he'd have caught it, anyway. Becca nudged his toe with hers, and when he looked up said softly, "Wave at Bill Platter and his wife. To your left."

Dan looked that way and lifted an arm in greeting before turning back to Becca. "Thanks. He coming over?"

"Nope. Heading for the car. They always go to her mother's in Waurika on Sunday."

Dan nodded, keeping his gaze glued to her face. "Graduated high school with Bill."

She lifted her eyebrows. "He looks older than you."

"He is. Held back, dropped out for a while."

"Is that so? Then you'll be surprised to hear that he's a big man around here now. Pretty well-heeled. Owns an insurance agency in Duncan."

His mouth quirked at the word *hear,* but she didn't apologize, sensing that would compound the mistake. "Surprised he's living in Rain Dance, then."

"How come? You're living in Rain Dance now."

He looked away, mumbling, "Inherited my house."

She stood silently until he glanced her way again. "Is that the only reason you came home, because you inherited your grandmother's house?"

He turned away as if he hadn't understood her, but then he turned back again and looked her in the eye. "Not sure. It is home."

She smiled. "Yeah. I feel the same way. I couldn't think of living anywhere else after Cody died."

He asked gently, "Not long ago?"

"Twenty-one months," she told him. "Just after I found out I was pregnant with CJ."

His eyes widened. "Must've been tough."

She nodded. "But we're managing. I'm even finally going to get my house fixed up."

He chuckled and tossed his keys lightly, signaling his intention to take his leave. "We'll see. Tomorrow."

"Tomorrow," she echoed, adding, "Look left again and acknowledge Effie Bishop."

Dan turned his head and smiled at the elderly woman, calling out in that same careful, measured way, "Good to see you again, Miss Effie." He looked back at Becca as he moved into the parking area and mouthed the words "Thanks. Again."

She smiled, waved and went in search of her family, marveling at how he handled himself. No one who didn't know him well would realize his predicament, at least not with her acting as his ears. She found a strange satisfaction in that, one she didn't much want to ponder.

Dan brought his white pickup truck to a halt behind Becca's old car and studied the sight before him. He shook his head and killed the engine, automatically pulling the keys. The truck was spanking new, with fewer than two hundred miles on it. He'd ordered it specially equipped as soon as he'd made the decision to move back to Rain Dance, but it had never seemed so plush or shiny as it did now, sitting in front of Becca Kinder's shabby little house.

The house didn't need repairs, he realized with dismay—it needed demolishing. The roof line was uneven, the shingles a patchwork of colors and type. Over the low porch it sagged dangerously, and he saw that one of the support poles had sunk through the rotted wood and past the untreated joist to the ground. The house itself was built atop a foundation of cement blocks placed about two feet apart, so the floor probably rolled like an ocean inside. Besides that, every inch of wood siding needed scraping and painting. Windowsills were buckled. The damage was such that he could tell she'd been living like this for a long time, and that knowledge pricked him, though he supposed that he should've expected it.

Despite running the only grocery store in town, the Kinders had always been poor as church mice. None of them, Cody included, had ever seemed to mind. Dan remembered his grandfather saying that John Odem was a good man who had no head for business, that he gave credit to everyone who asked and probably collected only a fraction of what was owed him. That apparently still held true, and while Dan admired the generosity and pleasantness of the Kinders, he couldn't help feeling a little irritated on behalf of Becca and the kids. No wonder she'd pressed him for help.

He got out of the truck and walked across the dirt yard to the porch, noting as he stepped up onto it that the floorboards were warped and broken. The whole thing would have to be replaced. The patched screen door opened and Becca stepped out, looking freshly scrubbed and smiling a happy welcome.

"It's nearly ten. I was getting worried you wouldn't show till after lunch."

"Your morning off," he pointed out. "Thought you might sleep in."

She waved that away. "I'm a morning person, always up with the dawn." She hugged herself. "I love it when the world's still and quiet, like I'm the only person awake anywhere."

He smiled, not because he identified—for him the world was always still and quiet, and he missed the bustle and racket of it keenly—but because she never bothered to police her speech with him. Becca was just Becca. Period. He liked that, admired it. In a funny way he was even grateful for it. She made him feel...normal. Whole. He reminded himself that he was neither.

"Come on in," she said before leading the way inside.

He followed with some trepidation and found himself standing in a living room that couldn't have been more than ten feet square. Poorly furnished with an old sofa, a small bookcase, a battered coffee table, a cheap floor lamp and a small television set on a wire stand so rickety that it leaned to one side, the place was shabby but spotless and cheerful.

Becca had obviously made a valiant effort. A colorful quilt covered the ratty sofa. Bright yellow ruffled curtains fluttered in the morning breeze. An oval, braided rag rug covered a significant portion of the torn linoleum floor, and sparkling beads had been glued around the edge of the yellowed lamp shade. The bookcase bulged with neatly stacked rows of paperback novels, children's storybooks and Bible study materials. Best of all were the framed photos hung artistically on the wall, so many that they almost obscured the faded, old-fashioned wallpaper, along with a homemade shadow box of dried flowers and a variety of in-expert coloring-book pages pinned up at Jemmy-height. Jemmy sat on the floor industriously work-ing on another while watching cartoons.

Becca waved him into another room. He glimpsed a sunny bedroom as he walked past an open doorway, then came to stand in the disaster that was her kitchen.

It looked like something straight out of the thirties, with a tired old propane stove, a tiny an-cient refrigerator, peeling wallpaper that exposed its rough backing, a shallow tin sink and virtually no cabinets. The only work surface was an old table that obviously functioned as eating space and stood over the slanted entry of an old root cellar. A pair of unfinished shelves comprised the only storage, and a single naked lightbulb provided the only il-lumination, since the window and possibly a door had been boarded over. To top it all off, the baby sat in a rusty high chair in the very middle of the floor, naked except for a diaper, his hair, face and chest smeared and sticky. With one hand he clutched the remains of a banana while rhythmi-cally banging a spoon on the metal tray with the other. When Dan caught his eye, the filthy little cherub offered him the piece of mushy banana. Dan pretended not to notice and quickly diverted his attention.

Becca reached out and removed the spoon from the baby's hand with a patient shake of her head. "Sorry about the racket." Realizing what she'd said, she put a hand to her head and, eyes twinkling, said, "Sorry for apologizing."

He found himself smiling. Although the place was an appalling wreck and he was just beginning to realize what a job he'd let himself in for, he couldn't do anything but smile. She was one of a kind, Becca Kinder, as natural and uncomplicated as a woman could get. Widowed much too young, she worked long hours at the store owned by her in-laws, obviously didn't have a penny to spare, lived in appalling conditions and still managed to be happy and make a warm if humble home for her two children.

He'd do what he could, of course. He wouldn't be able to live with himself if he didn't, though he realized in that moment that he would be getting something important out of it, too. Because just by being herself and by treating him as if he wasn't handicapped, as if he was someone to depend upon, as if he had something of genuine value to offer, she made him understand that it was so. Plus, he could make a real contribution. He *could* help her. To what extent he wasn't yet certain, but her life and the lives of her children would definitely be better once he was through here. She couldn't know what a gift that was, and even if he'd had the words to tell her, he doubted that he could express it sufficiently, so he just looked her in the face and asked, "Where were you wanting to start?"

She gave him a bright, brilliant, happy smile that lightened his heart. Then he felt something brush his hip and looked down to find his jeans decorated with mashed banana.

Chapter Three

"Oh! I'm so sorry! CJ, stop that!"

Becca grabbed a dishcloth from the edge of the sink and rushed to scrub at the banana smeared on Dan's jeans. He jumped back. She followed and scrubbed at him anyway, and he could tell that she was speaking but not what she was saying, as she was bent over, concentrating on the stain. He tapped her on the shoulder, and she suddenly looked up.

"Work clothes," he said with a shrug. "No big deal."

She frowned, but it turned into a smile as she turned to scrub her son. Dan thought it a wonder the little tyke's skin didn't come right off. She looked at him over her shoulder. Apparently she had enough experience at this sort of thing that she didn't need to see what she was doing in order to do it.

"This is all my fault," she said. "He didn't really want that banana, but I was trying to keep him occupied. He tends to hang all over me when I'm not working."

You should stay home, he thought, and then realized from the look on her face that he'd spoken aloud. He hastily added, "If—if you could."

She nodded. "But I can't. They stay with the woman who lives next door to John and Abby, so they're close to the store, and by juggling our schedules we make sure they aren't there more than a few hours a day. That's why the butcher counter isn't open all the time anymore."

Dan had actually wondered about it, and had decided that John Odem wasn't getting any younger and had probably cut back his hours for that reason. Now he knew that John wasn't taking it easy somewhere while his wife and daughter-in-law ran the store. These Kinders were a wonder, with all their good-spirited hard work and caring.

"When CJ's older," Becca went on, "I'll take them both into the store with me. John Odem's going to set up a playroom, and Jemmy can help watch her brother."

Dan smiled lamely. "Good plan."

"CJ's still clingy, though," she said. "He's at that stage, you know."

Dan didn't know. He didn't have the slightest

notion about kids. He'd always imagined that one day he'd find some girl and settle down to parenthood, but soldiering had kept him too busy to do anything about it, and then one day it had taken the possibility away from him.

He knew that he couldn't be a fit parent. His own childhood experience told him that. When he thought about all the times he'd been awakened in the dark of night by some bad dream or frightening noise and how his mom and dad had rushed to his side at his call, he understood his own inadequacy. Thinking about the times he'd tried some silly stunt and injured himself had forced him to admit that his inadequacy could put a child at real risk.

No, he didn't know about kids, and he probably never would know more than the basics, even though his baby sister was planning a fall wedding and would, presumably, one day make him an uncle. He had to believe that God had a reason for the way things had turned out, and maybe Becca was showing him what that reason was. The skills he'd learned at his grandfather's and father's knees seemed to be playing an important role in it. Carpentry had always been an enjoyable pastime for Dan. Working with his hands gave him a certain satisfaction. Maybe it was meant to be more.

A small, delicate touch fell on his shoulder, and he realized with a jolt that Becca was speaking to him, but he hadn't been paying attention.

''I thought we'd start in here with some plasterboard. If you could just get it on the walls for me, I think I could get it plastered and painted. I've been reading up on how to do it.''

He blinked and looked around the room. She'd been reading up on tape and bedding. ''I can take care of it,'' he said, bringing his gaze back to her face. ''All.''

Her relief was palpable. ''Oh, good. New plasterboard would patch up some of the holes.''

He made a mental note to check the insulation before he nailed up any drywall. He'd bet his bottom dollar that this place didn't have a lick of insulation.

''Of course, I'll be wanting cabinets,'' she was saying. ''Nothing fancy, you understand. They don't even have to have doors.''

He'd never build her cabinets without doors, but he just nodded.

''And I would love it if we could replace that nailed-over back door,'' she went on. ''I don't like not having more than one exit, you know?''

''For safety,'' he said, and she smiled.

''Now, this is the most important part,'' she said, reaching over to place her hand flat against the rough boards covering the outside wall. ''There's a window under here, too, and I've always figured it would be the perfect place for an air conditioner. Some summer nights it's just so hot out here that my babies can't sleep.''

His mind was racing. How in heaven's name had

they survived an Oklahoma summer without air-conditioning? It meant 220 wiring, though. No doubt the whole place would have to be rewired. He wondered if this old house even had a fuse box. He tried to pay attention to what she was saying even as his brain whirred with what was needed: insulation, wiring, window, door, light fixtures, probably plumbing. Plasterboard and cabinets were way down the line. He made himself concentrate on the movement of her mouth and was stunned to read what it formed next.

"Two thousand dollars isn't a lot, I know, but I can get together more as we go along. It ought to make us a good start, don't you think?"

Sensing her hope and her eagerness, he couldn't make himself say what was on the tip of his tongue. He told himself ruefully that before he'd lost his hearing and become unsure of his own speech, he'd probably have blurted out that a measly two thousand wouldn't get this one room into really livable shape. Now he just covered his dismay with a nod and asked to see the rest of the house, explaining carefully that he needed to see what was behind certain walls.

She led him on a full house tour, which didn't take long, even with the baby attached to her hip. He wondered if she was going to survive this child's infancy with a straight spine, since she seemed able to walk only at an awkward angle while lugging the great brick.

Her bedroom was in the same pitiful shape as the rest of the place, but the tiny bath and second bedroom had been added to the house sometime in the past few years and were structurally sound, at least. Unlike the papered walls in her room, he couldn't see daylight through cracks. No wonder she wanted drywall in the rest of the house.

When they reached the second bedroom she put the baby down for a nap in a wobbly old crib squeezed into the corner next to the low, cotlike thing apparently used by the little girl, judging by the ruffly pink spread. The baby wailed, his chubby face screwing up and turning dark red, but Becca just bent low and kissed him, patting his belly until he calmed and rolled onto his side. The child was still awake when she led Dan from the room, but if he kicked up additional fuss, Dan couldn't tell and she didn't let on.

Back in the living room, he sat down to talk over what was going to happen next. Dan felt a distinct catch in his chest as he began to marshal his thoughts. She had so little. If he told her what this place really needed, she'd no doubt be upset, but would still want to do what little could be done with the funds she possessed. He decided that, though he couldn't lie to her, she didn't have to be over-whelmed with all of it at once. Besides, he could save her some real money by simply using what he had on hand, like the base cabinets he'd pulled out of the garage apartment. He'd thought them too old-fashioned to use, but they were solid and about the right size. Originally he'd intended to recycle the wood, but, stripped and refinished, the cabinets would make a welcome addition to her kitchen, especially if he dressed them up with doors that he could build in his shop out back of the house. She need not know that they were used—or free. And he certainly didn't have to tell her that he would take no profit on this job. That was his business, after all.

Jemmy crawled up into Becca's lap as she waited patiently for him to speak, and he figured it was polite to at least smile at the child. She brightened noticeably when he did so.

"You're right," he told Becca, switching his gaze to her face. "Start in the kitchen."

She closed her eyes with obvious relief. "Then you'll do it? You'll take the job?"

He nodded, waiting until she opened her eyes again to speak, realizing a heartbeat later that he need not do so. She could hear, for pity's sake. "I will make a plan for you to approve."

"Oh, you don't have to do that," she said, still smiling. "Just do what you think best."

"Best to have a plan," he said, and she shrugged.

He rose. "Get my tape. Make some measurements."

She hugged the little girl and bowed her head to say something to her. Jemmy looked up, delight and wonder in her eyes, and clapped her hands. Then suddenly she came off her mother's lap, zipped across the small space that separated him from them and was suddenly standing on his feet, her arms wrapped around his legs in a childish hug. He could feel her breath on his jeaned thigh, the movement of her lips but he was too stunned to comprehend even that she was speaking until she glanced back at her mother and then turned her face up.

He caught the words *nice man* and *Mr. Dan.* He looked helplessly at her mom, but Becca just sat there smiling. With a lump the size of his fist in his throat he couldn't have spoken even if he'd known what to say, so after a moment he gently dislodged the child and went straight out the door. Only as he was looking through the toolbox fixed to the bed of his truck did he once again regain his composure.

He took the plan to the store for Becca to see. It was a scaled-back, highly simplified version of the one he'd worked on almost nonstop for the past thirty hours. Hand drawn on simple white notebook paper, it was really nothing more than a floor plan of her kitchen with the cabinets, door and window set in place. He'd listed the work to be done, but it was only a brief overview and included such uninformative items as Basic Wall Preparation, Electrical Upgrade and Plumbing Adjustment, along with Door Installation and Cabinet Installation.

As he'd expected, she cared only about the final result, asking, ''What color will the cabinets be?''

"Your choice. Paint or stain?"

She had to think about it, but then she shook her head. "Whichever is cheapest."

He shrugged.

"Which is simplest, then?"

"Paint."

She grinned. "I like yellow."

He chuckled. "Exact color later."

"When can you start?" was her only other question.

He checked his watch. If he could get to the building supply outlet in Lawton today, he could start work in the morning. "Tomorrow."

She clasped her hands together in front of her chest, and tears filled her eyes. Alarm shot through him.

"It'll take a while," he warned, but she shook her head happily.

"I don't care. It'll be started. You know what they say. Once begun, sooner finished."

She turned to the cash register and opened the drawer. Extracting an envelope, she turned back to him, then carefully placed it in his hands. He knew what it was even before he thumbed back the flap. She'd just handed him her life's savings in cash. Humbled, he quickly decided against trying to return it. Instead, he'd earn the trust she had just placed in him.

He left her a copy of the plan and drove straight to Lawton, some seventy-five miles distant. Surprisingly, he found a number of good sales, so the two thousand dollars bought him just about everything he'd need to get her kitchen into decent shape. It seemed that he wasn't the only one with a plan. He decided to let God worry about everything else.

It took him three days to get the kitchen wiring done, the new door and window framed in, the glass installed, the walls stuffed with pink fiberglass insulation and the longed-for plasterboard on the walls. Since the electricity had to be off, Becca and the kids stayed in town with her in-laws for a couple of nights, but by the time he got the door hung on the third evening she was there with both little ones and a bag of groceries in tow. She sent the girl back into the living room and gave the kitchen a careful look.

"I can't believe how much you've gotten done," she said, placing the bag on the table that he'd pulled across the floor and out of his way. "It's ready for the tape and plaster."

He nodded, feeling a spurt of pride. "Tomorrow."

She adjusted the baby on her hip and smiled, looking around the room. "I could help," she said, facing him.

He shook his head. "My job."

She sighed, but he saw the smile in her eyes. "Okay, if that's the way you want it."

"Yes."

"Hungry?" she asked, pulling a paper napkin from the bag and preparing to dust the tabletop. "I brought plenty. The least I can do is make sure you eat."

He'd brought a sandwich for lunch, but the aroma of roast beef was making his stomach rumble now. Deciding that it would be impolite to refuse her offer, he looked at his dusty hands and checked his wrist for the time. Sixteen minutes after seven! No wonder he was hungry.

"Better wash up," he said.

She nodded, and he moved toward the newly installed back door, picking his way around tools and scraps of building material. He felt something very light bounce off his back and stopped, turning. She pulled another napkin from the top of the bag. He looked at the wadded one on the floor, then back to her.

"Where you going?" she asked before starting to wipe off the tabletop.

"Spigot out back."

She lifted her eyebrows. "Why not use the bathroom?"

The bath was the most feminine room in the house, pink and flowery and as clean as a surgical suite. Cody had obviously added the room and the kids' bedroom onto the house himself and managed a fair job of it. No doubt he'd have had the whole place whipped into shape by now, had he lived. Instead, Dan was doing the work. It didn't seem right, and Dan was never more keenly aware of that than when he was standing in her little bathroom looking at her pink fixtures. He couldn't help wondering if Cody had installed them to please her. He certainly would have.

Shaking his head, he slapped at the legs of his jeans and said, "Too dusty." Then he escaped out the back door to bend over the rusty old faucet at the corner of the house. By the time he returned, Becca had unpacked a number of disposable containers from the bag, and the girl had dragged the high chair in from the living room, where he'd moved it.

Becca was talking, but he didn't try to follow her, his interest taken by the food as she opened the containers. He saw sliced brisket, baked beans, potato salad, coleslaw and a thick, rich barbecue sauce. She held up a bundle of butcher's paper and unwrapped it, displaying three large pickle wedges and small banana peppers. He reached for one of the pickles, mouth watering.

She inclined her head toward the root cellar. "There's bread in a box on the steps."

He bit off a hunk of the tart pickle as he moved to open the flimsy cellar door. Inside, about four steps down a steep flight of rickety stairs, sat a cardboard box full of foodstuffs that Becca had removed from the kitchen shelves the night before he'd started work. A plastic bag of sliced white bread lay on top. He stooped and picked it up by the wrapper. By the time he carried the bread back to her, Becca had set the table with paper plates and plastic forks.

Jemmy hopped up on one of the pair of available chairs, but Becca spoke to her, and she started getting down again.

"Stay there," Dan said, reaching for a short stepladder. It made a tall but adequate stool when he sat on top of it. Becca put the baby in his chair and sat down.

Four people seated around a rectangular table in the littered kitchen made for a very crowded room, but Becca's smile and his own satisfaction in a job progressing well overrode any awkwardness as Becca began filling plates. She piled his high, and he let her, suddenly ravenous. From pure habit he began to bow his head, then he felt a jolt as Becca took one of his hands in hers. Jemmy's little hand slid into the other. His gaze flew to Becca. She had bent her head but lifted it again, eyes closed, as she spoke a simple grace.

"Thank You, Lord, for all Your many blessings, family, home, this delicious food and especially for Dan and all the good things he's brought to us. We have need, Lord, and You've sent this fine man to help. Bless him for his willingness to share his talent."

Dan felt a kick inside his chest. A fine man. He inclined his head and silently asked God to make him worthy of that description. When he looked up again he saw that Becca and Jemmy watched patiently. He looked at Becca and followed the seemingly natural impulse to squeeze her hand. She smiled. It was like warm sunshine bathing the cluttered, half-finished room. She pulled her hand back and began eating. Jemmy did the same, so he dug in to his own food.

"Good," he said after swallowing.

She nodded and dabbed at her mouth with a napkin before saying, "John Odem cooks a couple times a week for the deli case. Monday it was a huge ham and macaroni and cheese."

Dan nodded. "I bought some. Real sweet."

"Yeah, he likes that brown-sugar-cured ham."

They concentrated on the meal for some time, then Dan noticed that Jemmy reached for one of the small yellow peppers on the butcher paper with the pickles. He shot a quick glance at Becca, who smiled and said, "She eats them all the time. John Odem again."

Dan chuckled and watched with interest as the little girl gingerly nibbled the succulent yellow flesh. "Hot?" he asked when she met his eyes.

She shook her pale head. "Nah, na if yont ea te sees."

"Not if you don't eat the seeds," he repeated carefully, realizing that she was eating around the ball of seeds inside the pepper. She nodded and kept nibbling. He felt an odd glow of pleasure. Children were often difficult to understand because they didn't always get words right, but he'd followed Jemmy. She was smart for her age, or maybe her diminutive size made her seem younger than she was. "How old are you?" he asked.

She grinned and held up four fingers, spouting rapid-fire words, few of which he caught this time. Lost, he looked to Becca, who ducked her head to hide a smile before lifting it again to say, "Jem's telling you that she had a party on her birthday, which is February tenth, and that you're invited next year. It's going to be here in our 'newed' house, by the way."

"Newed?" he repeated uncertainly.

Laughter danced in her soft green eyes. "Abby told her the place was going to be 'like new.' So in her mind when you're done it'll be 'newed.'"

He glanced at Jemmy and smiled. She beamed at him with something akin to hero worship. Just then something flew right past the end of his nose. He looked down to find a corner crust of bread on the table next to his plate. When he glanced in the direction it had come from, he noticed that both Jemmy and Becca were laughing. Even CJ, who had obviously launched the missile, judging by the white stuff oozing from his fist, was grinning broadly, showing off the few teeth he possessed.

"I'm sorry," Becca said. "He saw me throw the napkin to get your attention earlier."

Dan looked at the boy, and something in that little face seemed to be saying that he craved the same attention that Dan had been showing his big sister. Without even thinking about it, Dan picked up the scrap of bread and tossed it back at the boy. It was just long enough and just curved enough, incredibly, to hang on the boy's bit of a nose. For an instant Dan couldn't quite believe what had happened, and neither, apparently, could anyone else, but then the little imp grinned, put back his head and laughed so hard that his round little body jiggled all over. His whole being seemed to light up, even as he collapsed into the corner of the chair, laughing. The kid was so purely tickled, that crust of bread now clasped in his plump hand, that everyone was laughing, Dan included. He laughed so hard that his chest shook and tears gathered in his eyes. It almost hurt. He hadn't laughed like this, felt this good since…so long.

He wiped his eyes and looked at the smiling faces around him. It was time to be happy again, time to stop licking his wounds and concentrate on the good in life, on the good that he himself could do.

Chapter Four

"You don't have to keep feeding me," he said slowly.

Becca had noticed that when he spoke carefully and precisely, his tone often lacked inflection, but when he blurted out or tossed off words, his speech was almost normal. This sounded like something he had rehearsed, at least in his mind, and she wasn't at all surprised. They'd enjoyed several meals together in her quickly evolving kitchen, and though he often seemed pleased and relaxed, she had identified a growing unease, a certain tension developing between them.

"You have to eat," she said, making sure he could see her face as she laid out the food. "Besides, it's the least I can do. You're working long hours, and you can't be making much money on this job."

When she thought about the material he'd used so far, she wondered if he could be making any profit, especially considering those cabinets. Even without the doors, which he said he was still building, they improved the room a thousand percent. And then there was the cookstove, which he'd said was used. She had no reason to doubt him, except that he'd pretended not to see when she'd asked where he'd gotten it. She kept wondering if his garage apartment had an empty space where the cookstove used to be, and the idea made her cringe inside. She wasn't above a certain amount of charity, frankly, but even she had her pride.

"Don't need money," he said matter-of-factly, filching a potato chip from the open bag on the table. They were still eating deli food. She looked forward to the day when she could cook him a real meal.

"Everybody needs money," she replied.

He held up four fingers, counting off the reasons he didn't. "Medical disability. Military retirement. Inheritance. Good investments."

"And the rent on that garage apartment?" she asked.

"Soon," he said nonchalantly, averting his eyes.

She didn't let him get away with that. Reaching across the side chair that stood between them, she placed a hand flat against the center of his chest. He looked down at it, then slowly lifted his gaze to her face. "You can rent an apartment without a cookstove, then?" she asked pointedly.

He blinked and chewed. She lifted an eyebrow insistently. Finally he grinned. "Got a stove same place I got yours. Used. Dealer in Duncan."

She narrowed her eyes, thinking that he'd worded his reply rather oddly. "It's not the same one, then?" He shook his head. "You swear?"

His mouth quirked. "Never swear. Much. When I hit my thumb with a hammer, maybe." She laughed, and he grinned. "Not the same," he promised. "Honest."

She couldn't help noticing that his eyes crinkled in a most attractive way at the outside corners when he smiled, and for the first time she was truly glad that he couldn't hear the husky tone her voice had acquired. "I just don't want to take advantage of you, Dan—no more than I can help, anyway."

"I understand."

"I know you do. You're just such a blessing to us, and I can't tell you how grateful I am."

He shook his head. "I am blessed. You work hard." He poked a thumb at his chest. "I get checks in the mail."

"You deserve those checks," she told him, looking up into his chiseled face. He was a handsome man, with those blue eyes, and a good one, too. That much had become very obvious.

CJ banged on the metal high-chair tray, but she

ignored his bid for Dan's attention, keeping it all for herself.

"Maybe I do work a lot," she said, "but it's because I have to, and it's nothing compared to what you do out of the kindness of your heart." She thought of the clean white kitchen walls, the glass light fixture snugged against the stain-free ceiling, the door and the window where the compact air unit would soon be installed, the butter-yellow cabinets and mottled-gold countertop set with a white enamel double sink. After hanging the cabinet doors and connecting the stove to the propane, he was going to add shelves around the refrigerator and build a new cellar entrance set flat into the floor, since she needed the cellar space for additional storage and the floor space for the dining table. He intended to install new cellar steps, too, as well as strip, seal and paint the kitchen floorboards. After that he'd rip off the porch and build her a new one that she and the kids could actually enjoy. It was almost too much, and she felt tears gather in her eyes.

"Thank you," she whispered, going up on tiptoe to kiss his cheek. He needed a shave, and the delicate rasp of sandy whiskers lightly abraded her lips. She'd almost forgotten what it felt like to kiss a man's rough cheek.

Suddenly he whirled away and moved to the back door, but then he paused and looked over his shoulder. She couldn't read what crowded into those blue eyes. "Welcome," he mumbled, and slipped outside.

A moment later she heard the water running from the spigot in back of the house and looked ruefully at her new kitchen sink with its shiny faucet. Her fingers wandered up to touch her lips, and for a moment she wondered what it would be like to kiss Dan Holden on the lips, to be kissed by him.

A vague guilt pricked her. Was she being disloyal to Cody and the Kinders by thinking of Dan as more than an answer to prayer? Maybe she was more selfish and needy than she realized. She marveled at how much God loved people. For no reason she could understand He loved her enough to let her stumble across Cody, to bring her here to Rain Dance and the Kinders, to give her two healthy children and meet every one of her true needs. He'd even shown her joy and peace in the midst of heartbreak and loss. Was it asking too much, wanting too much to wonder if the pleasure that she found in Dan's quiet company might be more than fleeting?

Could God mean Dan Holden for her?

She was almost afraid to think it. But somehow she was more afraid not to.

Becca said a quick prayer as she twisted in her seat. She'd kept an eagle eye out for Dan Holden all morning, and through the tall, narrow church window she'd just glimpsed his lean form striding up the path toward the building. Her heart sped up, and she told herself sternly not to be a fool. She'd seen the man almost every day for the better part of two weeks now, ever since he'd started work on her house, and today would be no different. Except somehow it was.

They were great friends now, maybe even more. Or maybe they could be. She wasn't sure, frankly, though she'd prayed and prayed about it. Lately she'd wanted very much to talk to Abby about her feelings for Dan, but she hadn't dared. For one thing, Abby was her mother-in-law. For another, she didn't feel free to discuss a certain issue with Abby or anyone else. Dan's deafness was his business, after all.

Dan appeared in the doorway from the vestibule, and Becca bounced up to her feet, motioning for him to come forward and join her. He glanced around uncertainly, but then he started down the aisle, right past the place where he usually sat. She plopped down again and briefly closed her eyes with a mixture of relief and excitement before turning up a smile for him as he slipped into place beside her. Abby and John Odem leaned forward to offer their own smiles, which Dan returned with nods. Jemmy, however, fairly shouted, "Hello, Mr. Dan!" just as the organ started playing. Dan didn't see.

Becca nudged his knee with hers, mouthed Jemmy's name and gave her hand a little wave. Dan instantly looked at Jemmy, smiled and waved as the congregation rose to its feet. Becca opened the hymnal to the correct page. Then, mindful of his desire not to broadcast his disability, she moved it sideways so it would look as if they were sharing. His gaze dropped on her before shying away, even as his hand rose to help support the heavy book.

Standing shoulder to shoulder with him—well, shoulder to forearm—Becca quickly found her place, using the tip of her forefinger to locate the word with which she picked up the lyrics. Quite without thinking, she followed the words with her fingertip for several seconds as she sang, before two realizations hit her simultaneously. One, Dan was tapping his toe in time to the music. Perhaps he couldn't actually hear the sound of it, but he could feel the beat. And two, he was following the words to the song as she sang them by following the progress of her fingertip.

A feeling of deep satisfaction crept over her. It wasn't much of a service, really, nothing at all on the scale of what he was doing for her. Dan could read the words to any song for himself at any time, while she could never in a dozen years do what he had done to her house. But by helping him to follow along in time to the music, she felt that she was helping him join in somehow—not with the singing, but maybe with the praising. And wasn't that the most important part? Or was she searching for something that didn't truly exist, assigning more

significance to a simple courtesy than was war-
ranted?

They went through the remainder of the service
much as they had at Easter. Dan took his cues from
those around him and paid particular attention to
every word the pastor said, but this time Becca realized that he couldn't really catch each and every
word, for often the pastor turned his head or looked
down at his text or distorted words for emphasis.
Becca began to realize how confined Dan's world
had become, and she tried to think of ways in which
she might help him. She could record the sermon
and then repeat back every word to Dan in some
private place, or she could write it all out for him
to read at his leisure. That seemed to limit his par-
ticipation in the experience, but those were the best
ideas she had at the moment. She decided to discuss
the possibilities with him.

After the service, Becca kept pace with Dan until
they were out of the foyer. Then she grabbed his
arm and tugged him down a hallway, explaining,
"I have to get CJ."

He blinked at her, a question in his eyes. It was
the long way around to the nursery.

"I want to ask you something."

He nodded and kept his gaze on her face as they
hurried along the narrow corridor. She glanced
around to make sure she wouldn't be overheard and
said, "You're missing words during the sermon.

Pastor doesn't know to keep his head up when he's speaking.''

"Like you do," Dan said with a smile.

"I could help you fill in the blanks," she said, coming to a stop. Quickly she told him her idea for recording the sermon and speaking it back to him or writing it all out. He bowed his head, and she just hated it because she couldn't tell what he was thinking, but then he looked up again, and his smile and the blue of his eyes felt very soft.

"Becca," he said slowly, "I get enough of the sermon to fill in the blanks for myself."

"Oh."

"You don't have to find ways to pay me back."

"I'm not." She bit her lip. "Okay, maybe I am, but I just want to help."

He smiled. "You have. I needed to know *I* could still help someone."

She gaped at him. "Are you kidding? Why, if I had one tenth of the skills you do, I—"

"Wouldn't need me," he said, cradling her cheek with his palm. "I wouldn't have a friend." He grinned. "Not one who'd share her songbook."

Even as a warm glow suffused her, she whispered, "You'd have more friends if you'd just let everyone know—" He dropped his hand and looked away, effectively cutting her off. She realized only after he did that they were no longer alone. Two women were walking toward them, Amanda Cox and Jane Robertson, both Sunday-school teachers with classrooms on this hall. Becca tossed them a wave and headed for the nursery, Dan at her side.

When the nursery worker handed CJ over the half door, he surprised everyone by making a grab for Dan, who grappled awkwardly with him until CJ got an arm around his neck. Becca felt warmth flush into her cheeks.

"Come here, you," she said, reaching for her son. "Dan doesn't want to lug you around."

But CJ drew back from his mother. Dan hefted him in his arms as if getting a feel for his weight, and said, "I'll carry him."

"He's heavy," Becca warned needlessly.

"Like lead," Dan agreed, looking at the boy, who grinned at him around the finger in his mouth.

Embarrassed by her son's grab for Dan's attention, Becca took the diaper bag and hurried through the church to the front lawn, where Abby and John Odem waited with Jemmy. The friends with whom they'd been chatting broke off and moved away as Becca and Dan approached with the baby.

"Sorry to keep you waiting," Becca said. She slung the straps of the diaper bag over one shoulder and reached for CJ. "I'll take him now."

But Dan moved toward John Odem, saying to Becca, "He's too heavy for you."

John took the boy and parked him on a hip, quipping, "You're a little mountain, aren't you, boy?"

Abby was laughing. "You won't believe it, but

Cody was the same way. His age caught up with his size at about six.''

Dan nodded and said, ''Yes, ma'am,'' meaning he hadn't really caught what she'd been saying. ''You folks have a nice day,'' he added just a little too loud as he prepared to take his leave of them.

''Wait a minute, Dan,'' Abby said just as he turned away, and Becca quickly reached out to snag him by the arm. He glanced at her, then turned back to Abby as she said, ''Why don't you join us for dinner today? I've got a pot roast in the oven. It ought to be ready about the time I get the bread made.''

''Yeah, and nanner pudding,'' John Odem added, using Jemmy's word for banana. Dan was staring at Abby and didn't even know John had spoken.

Jemmy saw an opportunity to draw even with her brother on the attention scale and started hopping up and down pleading, ''Please. Please. Please.''

Dan looked at her and then at Becca, who was holding her breath. Suddenly he nodded.

''Thanks.''

Becca's smile broke free, even as she worried how he was going to pull this off. She wouldn't have him embarrassed or shamed for the world. Abby busily started directing everybody.

''John, get these kids in their car seats. Becca, you show Dan the way over. Jemmy, don't you step foot in the parking lot without holding your grandpa's hand.'' As she herded John and the kids toward their car, she said over her shoulder, "Dan, we could use some ice. That freezer in front of the store isn't locked."

"Come on," Becca said quietly, making certain he could see her face even as she moved to his side. "We have to stop by the store for a bag of ice."

He nodded and dug out his keys with one hand. The other just sort of naturally cupped Becca's elbow. She waved at a few folks as he handed her up into the passenger side of the truck, then took a look at the inside of the vehicle as he walked around to the driver's door. She noticed at once that the radio had been replaced by a flat black screen with tiny domed lights placed at intervals around its perimeter.

He settled behind the wheel, inserted the key into the ignition switch and began buckling his seat belt. Becca tapped his forearm, pointed to the black screen and asked, "What's this?"

"Global satellite positioning system," he said, starting up the engine so the thing would come on.

"That's like a moving map, isn't it?" she said, buckling her own belt.

He nodded and ran a finger around the lights, saying, "These let me know when there's a loud noise and where it's coming from."

"Like a siren or car horn."

"Like that," he confirmed.

"Cool."

He put the transmission in gear, looked over his

shoulder and backed the truck out of the space. Within seconds Becca saw that conversation would be difficult. He was a very attentive driver, which meant that he had to keep looking around him all the time, alert for what he couldn't hear and the alarm wouldn't recognize as important.

When he pulled up in front of the store, she unbuckled her belt and hopped out of the truck to hurry over to the freezer positioned next to the store entrance. She extracted an eight-pound bag of ice, carried it back to the truck and placed it on the floorboard before climbing in herself. As she was buckling her safety belt again, Dan asked, "Is that always open?"

"Sure."

"Anybody could take ice," he pointed out.

Becca shrugged. "Most folks will tell you next time they're in the store."

"Not all."

She shrugged again. He shook his head and drove the truck across the small parking lot to the street. "Turn left," she instructed. Realizing he couldn't have seen her, she reached across the wide bench seat, tapped his shoulder and pointed left.

He turned left. At the stop sign she pointed left again. He chuckled. "I know the way. Lived on this street."

"Oh."

Abby must have known that. So why had she told Becca to show him the way to the house? Her interest in Dan must be more obvious than she'd realized. Becca sat back and thought about Abby. It must hurt her mother-in-law to know that Becca was forming an interest in another man. Yet she'd invited Dan to Sunday dinner. Becca wondered what she'd ever done to deserve the Kinders and all the good things they'd brought into her life.

When Dan pulled the truck to the side of the street in front of the small, modest Kinder house, Becca started to get out, but he stopped her.

"You didn't tell them," he said, and she knew that he was referring to his deafness.

"Of course not." She picked up the bag of ice from between her feet. "But don't worry, I'll help you stay on top of the conversation. You'll have to stay close to me, though."

He looked at her, smiled and took the ice from her, saying, "Thanks."

Feeling some trepidation at the task ahead, she got out of the truck and joined him on the buckled sidewalk. Together they moved across the grass to the concrete steps that led up to the stoop and the door. With one last smile of encouragement, Becca opened the door and ushered him inside. The small, crowded living room was dark and cool. Becca quickly snapped on a lamp.

Abby appeared in the doorway to the kitchen, wearing an apron over her Sunday dress. "Come on in," she said, disappearing again. "John's changing the kids' clothes." Becca knew that she ought to help John get the children out of their Sunday clothes, but she dared not leave Dan on his own. He followed her into the kitchen, carrying the bag of ice.

"Where do you want this?" he asked.

Standing in front of the small, high table where she did most of her kitchen work, Abby stirred buttermilk into the depression she'd made in a bowl of flour and other dry ingredients as she answered him. "Just put it in the sink there, hon."

Becca pointed to the sink, but Dan didn't even look at her, let alone budge. Instead he just stood there holding the bag of ice by the end with one hand. Then he said, a little too loud, "You'll have to look at me when you speak to me, ma'am."

Abby did look at him then, obviously surprised, but no more so than Becca when he calmly announced, "I can't understand you if I can't see your mouth move. I'm deaf, Mrs. Kinder."

Becca clapped a hand over her heart, which had just given a decided lurch. Abby dropped the spoon into the bowl with a clatter.

"Oh, my soul!"

Dan looked down, then carried the ice to the counter and laid it gently in the sink, demonstrating that he had gotten Becca's message after all. Tears gathered in her eyes. He had obviously already made the decision to go public with his problem when he'd accepted Abby's invitation. Becca wanted to let him know how proud she was of him, and the only way she could think to do it without making a complete idiot of herself was with a touch. Slipping her hand into his, she briefly squeezed and retreated, but not before getting a quick squeeze back.

He leaned a hip against the old-fashioned, chrome-edged counter and folded his arms, facing Abby. "Should've told everyone sooner," he admitted. "Hard thing for a soldier who isn't one anymore."

Abby came around the worktable and enveloped him in a hug. "I'm sure glad you came home," she said.

Dan could obviously tell that she was speaking but couldn't know what she was saying, so he looked to Becca. She told him out loud what Abby had said so that Abby would know she hadn't made herself understood.

"She's glad you came home."

Dan smiled and hugged Abby back. "Me, too."

Just then Jemmy bolted into the room in her bare feet, wearing shorts and a T-shirt. "Mr. Dan, Mr. Dan! I gots a turtle in a box in the yard. Come see." As she spoke, she ran out onto the closed-in porch that served as a second bedroom. Becca called her back into the room, while Abby dabbed at her eyes with the hem of her apron.

"Honey, what have I told you about speaking to Mr. Dan?"

Jemmy looked up at Dan and asked politely, "Want to see my turtle? Please."

Dan smiled. "Sure."

"But not until you get some shoes on," Abby instructed.

Jemmy bolted for the porch again, crying, "They're under the bed. Mr. Dan can help me."

Becca caught her by the shoulders and turned her back to face Dan. "I'll help you with your shoes, but you have to remember to look Mr. Dan in the face when you speak around him."

"How come?" Jemmy wanted to know, not for the first time. Becca had always told her that it was the polite thing to do, but this time Dan went down on his haunches next to Jemmy and told her the truth.

"I have to read the words on your lips because I can't hear."

She checked briefly to be sure his ears were where they should be and repeated her question. "How come?"

"A big boom damaged the nerves in my ears. It was so loud it knocked me out of the room, which was underground, and put me to sleep for a long time."

"How long?"

"Two days."

Jemmy's eyebrows went up. "How come you were under the ground in a room? Was it a storm?

Sometimes we might go to the cellar if a bad storm comes."

"I was looking for bombs." He glanced up at Becca and added dryly, "Found some."

She bit her lip to keep from laughing, because it really wasn't funny.

"Why were you doing *that?*" Jemmy wanted to know.

"It was my job," he said simply. "I was in the military."

"What's miltry?"

"A soldier," Becca explained.

Eyes rounding, Jemmy blurted to Dan, "You're a soldier?"

"I was," Dan answered. Then he looked up at Becca and said, "Now I'm a carpenter."

"Like Jesus!" Jemmy announced importantly.

Knowing he'd missed that, Becca waved his attention back to her daughter.

"What?"

Jemmy said, "Jesus was a carpenter. He made chairs and crosses and stuff."

Dan smiled. "That's right."

Abby suddenly shoved a paper towel full of pieces of cabbage at Becca, saying thickly, "Ya'll go on and tend that turtle while I get my bread in."

Knowing that she was anxious to have a good cry in private on Dan's behalf, Becca nodded and turned Jemmy toward the porch. Dan rose and followed.

Like the rest of the house, the porch-become-bedroom was cramped and faded, much as it had been when Cody had slept here on the full bed as a boy. Dan took that all in before turning to pay indulgent attention to Jemmy who babbled about her turtle while Becca wrestled shoes onto her feet.

Those shoes would have to be replaced soon, as Jemmy was outgrowing them, but Becca couldn't worry about that now. It was a beautiful spring Sunday in Oklahoma, and the world felt bright and glorious, especially as Jemmy blossomed and preened for Dan.

It struck Becca then how much her little girl missed her father. John Odem did his best to fill in, but it wasn't the same as having a daddy to poke twigs at your turtle and smile as you tried to impress him with what a responsible pet owner you were. Becca had been too busy to notice how hungry her children were for male attention, but as always, God had seen the need. And sent Dan Holden.

Chapter Five

Crouched over a patch of sand with Jemmy, Dan enjoyed the sunshine as he watched the little girl feed bits of cabbage to her turtle. He felt lighter somehow, breathed easier, as if a weight had been lifted from his chest.

Apparently a previous owner had written the turtle's name, Buddy, on its back with a black marker, and Jemmy had suffered through weeks of worrying that the writer would return to claim the animal. During that time the Kinders had posted a sign in their store window, much as people often did for stray cats and dogs. Dan had smiled when he'd seen it.

Found—Turtle
Doesn't answer to the name Buddy.

Jemmy petted the hard shell, watching with satisfaction as her silent companion munched at the pale green hunks of cabbage. Turtles had always struck Dan as stoic creatures, but every time Jemmy brushed her fingertips over the turtle's back little Buddy closed his eyes, looking for all the world like a turtle that had found a piece of turtle heaven. Maybe he himself had been a little bit the way he'd imagined turtles to be: slow, unemotional, silently enduring a lonely existence. Now, for some reason, he felt a kinship with this little fellow.

Dan wondered where the turtle's original owner might be. Surely anyone in the area would have seen Jemmy's sign. There wasn't another grocery store for miles around, and a turtle couldn't have traveled far on its own. Could it? Maybe he and Buddy were more alike than he even knew.

Have you been around the world, Buddy? Dan wondered. Did you travel far away and somehow find your way home again, like me?

He felt a tap on his shoulder and looked up at Becca.

''Dinner's ready.''

He nodded and stood to watch as Jemmy carefully transferred Buddy to his cardboard box house with holes cut in the sides. She placed the box, with a bed of yellow grass and a large bowl of water inside, beneath the shade of an oak tree.

Becca waved Jemmy forward, then followed her into the house. She said something to the child, who nodded and rushed on into the kitchen. "You'll want to wash up, too," Becca said, turning to him. "You can use the kitchen sink as soon as Jemmy's done." She followed the child, presumably to be sure that she washed her hands sufficiently.

The instant he stepped up into the house, a mélange of rich, complex aromas tickled his nostrils and made his stomach rumble in anticipation. While he waited for his turn at the sink, he looked around the back porch. It had been sealed off with heavy plastic sheeting and plywood to make a bedroom, with a metal rod hung across one end for a closet. Atop that rod and the odds and ends of clothing that hung from it lay a battered old tan felt cowboy hat that Dan recognized as belonging to Cody, a memento of the boy he had been. That hat said to Dan that the Kinders were irrefutable proof that happiness wasn't about things or money—not that he'd ever really believed that. Still, he'd always had nice things and plenty of money to buy more if he needed or wanted. He had good parents and wouldn't wish for any others, but he couldn't help feeling a little envious of Cody at the moment. How simple and fulfilling his life must have been.

Simple, fulfilling and short, Dan reminded himself as Becca beckoned him. While he washed up, she helped Abby carry food to the table. With his hands clean and dry, he moved out into the space that served as the dining area. It was nothing more really than an awkward corner at the end of the living room where doors from all the other rooms in the house—bedroom, bath and kitchen—could swing open without colliding, but Abby had managed to tuck a round, claw-foot table and a number of mismatched chairs into it. Obviously no doors could be opened when the table was occupied, so the kitchen door had been removed from its hinges. John Odem was already sitting at the table when Dan arrived, with CJ propped up by pillows and tied with a dish towel to a chair beside him. A space equal to the boy's reach had been cleared on the tabletop. Deprived of more interesting utensils, he smacked the table repeatedly with his hands.

John Odem said something and pointed to a chair across the table from him, but Dan was uncertain if it was meant for him or someone else until all the females moved to other chairs. He waited until Abby, Becca and Jemmy were seated before pulling out the chair and sitting down. He positioned himself and scooted up to the table. The cushion felt a little lumpy and uncertain, but he didn't let that bother him—until he looked up and saw that everyone was staring at him.

Suddenly Abby glared at John Odem. Obviously scolding him, she shook her finger, speaking furiously. Unsure what was going on, Dan looked at Becca.

''John Odem's a great prankster,'' she explained with a wry smile, ''and this time he meant to pull a trick on you, but the joke's on him.'' She moved her gaze to John and told him what Abby apparently had not.

"Didn't hear?" John said. "How could he not hear that?"

Abby apparently spelled it out for him. John's mouth gaped open so wide that Dan began to fear his upper denture would fall out. Then John smacked his knee and began to laugh. The old man howled until tears ran in rivulets down his craggy face.

It certainly wasn't the sort of reaction Dan had expected, but it all began to make sense when Becca said, "There's a whoopee cushion under the seat pad of your chair."

A whoopee cushion. Dan rolled onto one thigh and thrust a hand beneath the pad tied to the chair, extracting a small, collapsed bladder with a nozzle on one end. John Odem went off again, and this time Dan joined him.

Abby rose from her seat and snatched the thing from Dan's hand, her face red with embarrassment. She took the carving knife to it, sawed right through the rubber, and as she worked she lambasted poor old John Odem. Dan could see her jaw working but not what she was saying. Whatever it was, John took it all in stride, laughing at himself as easily as he'd laugh at anyone else.

The situation was pretty darn funny, and laughter, it turned out, seasoned a meal to perfection.

* * *

Dan shook his head regretfully, looking down at the easy chair John had invited him to take after turning on a basketball game on the TV. "Put me right to sleep," he explained. Catching the wave of Abby's hand from the corner of his eye, he turned to her.

"We don't mind if you take a little nap, Dan."

He smiled. "You ought not, after all that good food." He patted his middle.

"Well, then, stay and take a snooze," Abby insisted.

"Have to go, but thank you." He walked across the room and kissed her cheek, explaining, "I talk to Mom on Sunday. She'll worry if I'm late."

Abby nodded and patted his shoulder. "You go on then, son, but you come back again real soon."

"Yes, ma'am."

She turned and spoke to Becca, who ducked her head and moved to open the front door for him. He wasn't certain what had been said until they stepped out onto the stoop and she pulled the door shut.

"I was told to show you out." He smiled his understanding. She tilted her head to one side. "Can I ask you something?" He nodded. "How do you 'talk' to your mom?"

"E-mail. Chat online."

"Oh. Of course. So you don't have a phone, but you do have a phone line."

"For the computer and security system. For emergencies."

"That's good."

He wrinkled his nose and admitted, "My parents worry."

She smiled. "I understand."

"I know." He swept his gaze over her face and said simply, "Thank you."

Her eyes held his for a long time before they slid away. "It wasn't as hard to tell Abby and John as you thought it would be, was it?"

"No." Now that it was out in the open, he found that he was glad.

She wrapped her arms around herself as if suddenly chilled, and he felt the impulse to put his own arm around her, pull her close to his side. He looked away to gather himself, but her clean scent lingered. When he looked back, Becca asked, "Will I see you tomorrow?"

He hadn't worked the past Monday, figuring she needed some peace and quiet on her day off. Besides—and it was the oddest thing—as comfortable as her company often was, she made him uneasy, too.

"Summer's coming," she pointed out when he hesitated. She didn't have to say that the heat would make her and the kids miserable and the outside work unbearable for him.

He didn't hesitate any longer. "I'll be there."

She brightened. "Good."

He saluted her with a little wave and went down the steps, pausing at the bottom to remove his keys from his pocket. It had been a lovely afternoon—relaxed, funny, companionable. He'd felt a part of something again, more at home than with his own family, who tried to hide their pain at his loss with well-meaning smiles.

Feeling a tug on his pant leg, he looked down to find Jemmy at his knee. She'd gone outside to tend her turtle the instant she'd been excused from the dinner table, but had apparently made her way around the house in time to catch him before he left. She crooked her tiny finger at him, and he dutifully bent low to read her words, but to his surprise, she just wrapped her thin little arms around his neck and hugged him tight.

For a moment he couldn't breathe, but it had nothing to do with the stranglehold Jemmy had on him. For an instant he knew what it would be like to have a child of his own, a fragile little person who loved without reserve. He felt a sharp pang of regret, and then she pulled free and ran back to her beloved turtle. Dan blinked, put properly in his place one rung below Duddy. Then he stood and caught the look in Becca's soft green eyes.

Suddenly he knew that his feelings for Becca were becoming complicated, even more so because they seemed to be reciprocated. Surely she wasn't looking at him as a new daddy for her children. That wouldn't do. He could never do the things that real fathers did, or even fit husbands, for that matter.

Troubled, he turned and went on his way.

* * *

Dan woke before the sun and fought back the impulse to dash straight out to Becca's. He dressed in lightly starched jeans and a soft, drab green, military-issue T-shirt, the tail neatly tucked in, and tugged on his comfortable lace-up work boots, no longer shined to a spit-polish gleam. After taking his time shaving, he scrambled some eggs and made a pot of coffee for breakfast. Even after that, it was still too early to go out to Becca's, so he thumbed through the local, county-wide newspaper.

Increasingly restless, he prowled the house after he finished the paper, but the emptiness and silence seemed unusually oppressive. He'd almost forgotten what a lonely world it was without sound to fill it: the tick of a clock, the hum of a ceiling fan lazily circling overhead, the ring of a telephone or doorbell… Funny he should think of those things now after all these months.

Desperate to keep busy, he turned on the TV set, but morning television couldn't hold his interest, and he couldn't seem to settle down to serious reading. He decided to go through the toolbox in the bed of his truck, reorganize things a bit. That was good for a long while, at the conclusion of which Dan figured he had the neatest toolbox for miles around. He glanced at his wristwatch. Eight o'clock. Still too early to show up for work on Becca's day off.

He opened the hood of the truck and checked all the fluids, then he checked the air pressure in all the tires and even swept out the floorboard and shook the mats. Finally he stacked the carefully painted cabinet doors in the bed of the truck, making sure to cushion them with an old quilt, and climbed behind the wheel.

It was just after nine when he pulled up in front of Becca's house. Barely had his feet touched the ground when the screen door flew open and Jemmy tore out of the house wearing a flowered cotton nightgown with a ruffle around the hem. She barreled straight into him, threw her arms around his legs in an exuberant hug and began jumping up and down, talking all the while. She caught his hand and pulled him toward the house. Surprised, he could only wonder if something had happened to Becca or CJ. Scooping Jemmy up into his arms, he literally ran toward the house, only to see Becca calmly step out onto the porch in cutoff jeans and a faded yellow blouse with the tail tied at her waist.

"What's going on?" he asked, hoping his panic didn't show.

She sipped from the glass of orange juice in her hand, smiled and told him, "You've been invited to breakfast with Jemmy and her dolls. She was worried you wouldn't get here in time."

He smiled with relief, though he had reservations. Jemmy had adopted him into the family, but she didn't understand what problems came with him. Framing his face in her small hands, she turned it so he could see her speak.

"It's a breakfast party in my bedroom and we got strawberries with cereal and juice."

He thought of his father sitting at a child-sized table, pretending to drink tea from toy cups while his sister babbled imaginary conversations with her dolls, and his heart squeezed. Setting Jemmy on her feet, he said, "Had breakfast," and quickly turned back to the truck.

How Jemmy took that or what Becca might have said to her once his back was turned, he couldn't know and wouldn't think about. Some distance was needed here, and yet he hadn't been able to think about anything else this morning except seeing Becca and the kids again. Just looking at Becca, all clean and fresh, made regret clench in his gut. He shouldn't have come today, but it was too late to make excuses and go.

Grimly determined to be strong in this, Dan hauled his tools into the house and set to work. He had cabinet doors to install, a floor to scrape and a full box of inexpensive self-stick vinyl tile to lay down before he could say that the kitchen was finished and get at that porch. He got busy, as near blind to the goings-on around him as he could make himself and still get the work done. It was easy to tune out, really, with no sound to distract him and the precise placement of hinges and handles to absorb him. He worked steadily but swiftly, step by logical step, measuring, marking, drilling, placing, setting, tightening until every screw in every hinge on every door was in its proper place.

The cabinets looked fine, 1,000 percent improvement if he did say so himself, but the work was nowhere near being finished. He went down on his knees and began scraping the ancient linoleum away from the floorboards with a spackling trowel, which he'd sharpened for the job. When he felt something touch the sole of his boot he warily moved into a crouch, pulling one foot up beneath him, and looked over his shoulder.

Becca was standing barefoot among a scattering of screws from a box he'd left on the seat of a chair he'd pulled away from the table to serve as a kind of workbench. In her arms she held baby CJ, red faced and wailing as she pried screws out of his fists. Realizing at once that the one-inch screws were small enough to be swallowed, Dan shot to his feet.

"He okay? Any in his mouth?"

Becca jostled the crying baby while using her thumb to force his chin down and get a look inside his mouth. She turned a calm face to Dan. "No, I don't think he'd gotten that far with them."

But he could have. The hair rose on the back of Dan's neck. That baby could have swallowed a whole box of screws. And Dan would've had to stumble over him to even know. Incredibly, he watched *her* apologize.

"He shouldn't have been in here. Jem spilled her cereal and I was distracted with…"

Dan turned away. He knew it was rude, but he just couldn't bear to let her apologize for his failings. Another man would have heard the child there. This only reinforced his resolve to keep his distance.

Disappointment hit him, as profound and deep as on the day he'd finally understood that he was never going to hear again. On that day he'd sat through an awkward consultation with his doctor conducted almost entirely in writing, then he'd gone quietly into his hospital room and sobbed, only to look up and find that a nurse had entered without his knowledge. That had seemed the crowning humiliation and a harbinger of what his life was going to be like from that point on. Turning his back on that embarrassed nurse had been his only option that day. Getting away from Becca was all he could think to do now.

"Done for the day," he announced, and started gathering up his gear. He dumped what he could into his portable toolbox, slapped the drill case under his arm, grabbed the flat metal squaring tool and headed for the door. Becca caught him by the arm as he passed her. Her small hand fit perfectly into the bend of his elbow and sent heat radiating up and into his chest. He forced himself to look at her face, seeing distress—and understanding. He felt bare, naked, raw. Whatever he expected her to say, it wasn't what he read on her lips.

"The cabinets look wonderful."

He nodded and pulled away before she could say more, moving quickly through the house and out to his truck. He didn't stop moving until he was once more safely behind the door of his own home. Just him. And the silence.

Chapter Six

Becca settled the baby more comfortably on her hip and sighed as she stared through the screen door at the level new floor of her porch and the empty road beyond. It had been days since she'd laid eyes on Dan. He was invariably gone when she got home in the evenings. Obviously he was avoiding her, and she didn't know why. She suspected that it had to do with the kids, even though that didn't make much sense to her.

Right up until Monday he'd been patient to the point of indulgence with them, but she was beginning to wonder if it didn't have more to do with his natural politeness and his circumstances than with Jemmy and CJ themselves. When Dan gave you his attention, it was necessarily intense. The lack of hearing and his dependence upon lipreading required him to lock his gaze on you, and the piercing blue of his eyes made the contact almost tangible. Unfortunately, a child wouldn't understand that such focus might not be personal. From Jemmy's and CJ's ends, the connection went right down to the core of their own need.

She hadn't realized how much they wanted a daddy. Even now Jemmy's memories of her father were pale, like a movie on a fuzzy TV. CJ had no memories of him at all. He was born into a world without daddies, at least as far as he knew. Yet he worked as hard for Dan's attention as Jemmy did, driven by some innate craving for a father figure.

Though while they both naturally gravitated to Dan, he continued to hold some part of himself aloof. From everyone. Oh, at times she'd sensed the possibility of more between Dan and herself, a deeper knowing, a magnificent sort of emotional connection, but circumstance had made him an artist at pulling back into himself, and he had definitely pulled back from her and the kids.

Maybe she'd read him all wrong. Maybe he just didn't like kids and was too polite to say so. And maybe it had more to do with the shock and self-condemnation she'd seen in his eyes when he'd realized that CJ had gotten into that box of screws.

She sighed again and turned away from the door. The half-finished porch depressed her.

Oh, it was lovely how he'd squared it up with the front of the house. For the first time the floorboards were neat and level. The corner posts rested not on the ground itself but on a foundation of cement blocks, which had in turn been set on footings of gravel laid into a trench hardened with lime. He'd even built a skirt around the lower edge of the floor so critters couldn't set up housekeeping underneath. Once a skunk had gotten in there and made the house unlivable for nearly a month. She wouldn't have to worry about that happening again. But without the shelter of the roof, the incomplete porch made the house feel abandoned and hopeless in a way that the old, rickety one never had. It made *her* feel abandoned and hopeless.

Foolish notions, she told herself. No child of God was ever hopeless. She was proof of that, and Dan Holden was part of it. He'd come just when she'd needed him most, just when her faith in her ability to provide a stable, comfortable home for her children had begun to waver. She couldn't shake the notion that the timing had been as right for him as for them. Hadn't he said that he'd needed to be needed, to know that his life had purpose and value?

He had more purpose and value than he knew, because the fact was that she missed him. She missed his steady, pleasant manner, even his terse conversation and that air of wounded pride, for if Dan Holden had anything in abundance it was pride. Considering that fact, she wondered how he managed to cope with his handicap at all and suspected that it was only by the grace of God and his own deep faith.

Perhaps that faith was why she felt a serenity with Dan that she'd never known with Cody, whose exuberant personality had brought fun and adventure into her life, but little peace. Cody's own belief had been sincere and absolute, but his happy-go-lucky nature had not lent itself to serious contemplation, and she had the feeling that Dan had done a whole lot of that, at least since he'd lost his hearing.

They did have one thing in common, Cody and Dan. They were both strong, masculine men who somehow made her keenly aware of her femininity without making her feel weak or foolish, as her father and brothers often had. She hadn't realized how important that was until she'd lost it. Now she could have a chance for that again, with Dan, if only he felt the way that she did. She just didn't know. She didn't even know how to find out. Abby always said that the only thing to do when a body didn't know which way to go was to get down on your knees, so that's just what Becca did.

By Sunday she was certain that God didn't mean her to give up on Dan Holden yet.

Once more she watched and waited for him, and when he finally appeared in church she summoned her nerve and signaled for him to join her, but Dan pretended not to see and reverted to his old pattern, taking a seat in the back pew and slipping out before anyone could engage him. She realized that she was going to have to force a confrontation, but it wasn't until after dinner that Becca decided to visit him at his house again.

She looked at Abby, who'd just mentioned that she was going out back to sit in the shade with Jem, and simply said, "I'm going to Dan's."

Abby's smile communicated understanding. "I was wondering how long you'd let it go."

"I don't want to push, but I have to do something. He just suddenly pulled back, and I don't even know why."

Abby nodded and patted her cheek. "You're good for him. That much is plain."

"Not to him, apparently."

"Well, maybe somebody needs to set him straight."

"I'm not sure anyone can."

"God can, if He wills."

"But I'm the one who has to talk to him," Becca pointed out.

"I'll say a prayer for you," Abby promised.

Becca smiled, hugged her mother-in-law and went out.

Not until she was halfway across the front yard did she decide to walk. It was only about a half mile to the Holden place, and she needed the time to gather her thoughts. She'd reasoned out a calm, careful approach that went right out of her head the instant she realized that a strange car was parked in front of Dan's house. She almost turned around, but it was too late for that. Dan was on the porch with two visitors, and she'd already been seen. Dithering for a moment, she didn't know what to do, whether to wait until the couple left or interject herself into the situation. Then one of the visitors, a woman, turned and smiled at her. A moment later Dan lifted a hand and waved her forward.

Becca felt embarrassed and horribly conspicuous as she moved up the walkway and climbed the porch steps, but then she noticed that Dan was speaking to the strangers in sign language. Intrigued, Becca moved closer. Dan rested his hands on his hips for a moment and gave her a look that said he didn't quite know what to do with her before quickly beginning to sign again. This time, he also spoke.

"Linda, Max, meet Becca." He spelled out her name, his fingers flashing the symbols at lightning speed.

The woman, a tall, thin brunette, looked at Becca with palpable interest. "Hello," she said warmly, her hands casually interpreting her words into sign language. "It's nice to meet you."

"I'm sorry to intrude," Becca apologized. "I didn't realize Dan had company."

"Oh, we're on our way out," Linda said, continuing to sign. "Max and Dan became friends in therapy last year, and we just wanted to stop by on our way home to Oklahoma City and see how he's doing.''

Becca looked at Max. "That's nice."

Linda signed for Max and said to Becca, "My husband doesn't read lips very well. He doesn't have the knack, and since he cannot speak, we communicate by sign language."

"I see."

Max spoke to his wife with his hands, and Linda turned to Dan. "We really have to be going," she said, leaning in to kiss his cheek.

"Good to see you," Dan told her.

Then he signed something and shook Max's hand as Max smiled and nodded and Linda said to Becca, "I hope we'll see you again sometime."

"That would be nice."

Just before they started down the steps, Linda looked back over her shoulder. "I'm glad Dan's doing so well."

"Very well, I think," Becca said, glancing at Dan.

He lifted a hand in farewell to his friends, then took Becca by the elbow and steered her unceremoniously into the house. The instant they were out of sight and earshot, he backed up about three steps and folded his arms.

"What?"

Becca bit her lip. Now that the moment had arrived, she wasn't sure how to begin, so once more she dithered. "I—I didn't realize that you had company."

"Even *I* have friends," he said, managing to sound sarcastic.

"Well, of course you do," she snapped. Bowing her head, she tamped down her impatience before looking up again. "They seemed very interesting people. I take it you were in therapy with Max?"

"Took therapy *from* Max."

"The sign language."

"Yes. Not everyone can lip-read. Max was born deaf."

"I see."

"He doesn't miss sound," Dan went on. "Never knew it."

"So he doesn't feel sorry for himself," Becca reasoned, realizing belatedly what she'd implied. "I didn't mean that you do."

Dan parked his hands at his waist and changed the subject. "Something wrong?"

"You tell me."

He made a face, as mute as his friend Max.

Becca licked her suddenly dry lips and looked around the neat foyer, taking in the large, lovely house even as she tried to find the right words to begin what promised to be a difficult conversation. Her house, in comparison to this, was a tumbledown shack, and the Kinders' wasn't much better. Dismayed by that knowledge, Becca searched for some way to reconnect with this man who had somehow lodged himself inside her heart.

"Would you teach me sign language?"

Dan stared at her for a full fifteen seconds before saying flatly, "No."

"Why not?" At last the words tumbled out. "What's gone wrong between us, Dan?"

He blinked and frowned. "Nothing."

"You know that's not true."

He shrugged as if to say that he didn't know what she wanted from him.

"You're avoiding me," she accused, "and I don't even know why."

Bowing his head, he brought his hands to his hips and said slowly, "Becca, it's best."

Flexing her fingers, she fought to keep her hands relaxed at her sides and waited until he looked at her. "I don't believe that."

Suddenly he threw up his hands. It was the first time she'd heard him shout, and she covered her ears, knowing that he couldn't realize how loud he was. "I'm not fit for you!"

She stomped forward, making him look at her. "That's not true."

"It is!"

Wincing, she automatically covered her ears again, then dropped her hands almost at once, but not before a look of sheer agony came over him.

"I can't even hear myself! People stare when I'm

too loud. Don't fit in. A freak.'' He closed his eyes. ''Easier alone.''

Her hands at his shoulders, she shook him until his eyes popped open. ''You're not a freak.''

''Not a whole man.''

''That's crazy.''

''Not the man for you.''

''How could you possibly know that? You haven't even given us a chance to find out!''

He leveled his gaze and enunciated each word carefully. ''You're a mother. I can never be a father.''

So that was it. She felt an odd sense of relief. It wasn't her, then. It was his fear of inadequacy. ''You think you can't be a father because you can't hear. That's baloney.''

He shook his head, an agonized look on his face. It was the same expression he'd worn the day that CJ had gotten into that box of screws. ''Kids get hurt, cry for help. If my child were in danger, I wouldn't know!''

''That was my fault with the screws,'' she told him, ''and I can hear just fine. There must be ways to minimize the risks.''

''Can't think of any. I've tried!''

Stepping closer, she looked up into his face. ''Things have a way of working themselves out if you just give them a chance.''

He swallowed and said, ''I have to accept my limitations.''

"And sometimes you have to at least try to move beyond them," she countered.

He shook his head stubbornly. "Not fair to the kids, you."

"Your deafness is not a problem for us. So you can't hear, so what?"

"So what? CJ almost swallowed screws. I didn't know!"

"You couldn't be expected to."

"My fault," he insisted stubbornly.

"Next time you won't leave them in reach."

Dan shoved a hand over the top of his head and said desperately, "I don't get half what Jemmy says."

Becca reached up and placed her hand in the hollow of his shoulder just above his collarbone. "Dan," she told him, "what you hear with your ears isn't nearly as important as what you say with your heart. Think on that, will you? And while you're at it, think on this." Going up on tiptoe, she angled her head and brought her mouth to his.

For an instant she thought he would pull away, but then his arms came around her, and for a brief, sweet moment she knew the joy of being held again, of being wanted again. Suddenly she remembered that she had instigated this, that he was too polite to do anything but kiss her back, and chagrin at her own forwardness made her break away. Appalled at what she'd done, she turned tail and left without even a word of farewell.

* * *

Dan was loading his tools into the back of the truck when Becca drove up to the house with the kids. She parked the car, got out and looked at him frankly, letting him know that she was surprised to find him still there. He was surprised himself, but he couldn't deny that he'd wanted to see her again. He'd missed her, much more than was wise, since she'd come to his house four days ago, since she'd kissed him. He stopped what he was doing and watched as Becca moved to the back door of the car and reached inside to free the children from their safety restraints.

Jemmy piled out first, pushing past her mom to reach the ground. She stood leaning against the car fender, watching Dan warily, her bottom lip stuck out. He felt like the biggest heel in the universe, but he didn't know yet what to do about it. He was so afraid of doing the wrong thing, the selfish thing.

Closing the toolbox, he waited for Becca to speak. She approached with CJ on her hip, moving in that twisted, leaning gait that she somehow made look graceful and natural. She studied the completed porch before switching her gaze to his face.

''Looks great.''

He nodded and let the feeling of a job well done flow over him. ''It'll look better painted.''

''Is that next?''

He nodded. ''Then walls and air conditioning.''

''So the cool air doesn't go right out the cracks,'' she surmised correctly.

He grinned. "Cheaper that way."

She looked down. He wanted to put his arms around her, but he didn't dare. That kiss was never far from the surface of his thoughts. He still didn't know how his arms had come to be around her or how he had lost himself so completely in the simple meeting of their mouths, but it was just one more danger in what felt like a whole minefield of possibilities that surrounded this woman.

She looked up again after a moment and suggested, "You could stay for supper."

He frowned and said, "Crock-Pot's on." It was the absolute truth. He'd put in a frozen chicken that morning. Only now did he realize that he'd done it to protect himself from staying to supper.

"All right, then," she said before looking over her shoulder at Jemmy.

"She okay?" he asked, concerned by the manner in which the child hung back.

"She's upset because I wouldn't let her have ice cream before we headed home. She'll be done pouting soon."

He tried to look at Jemmy without being too obvious about it. Was she crying over there? He couldn't tell in the waning light, and he didn't think it wise to get into the middle of a mother-daughter spat, so he stayed where he was, although it felt wrong somehow.

"Better go," he said, moving to the driver's door of the truck.

When he looked back at her, she said, "I wish you'd stay."

He sent his gaze skittering off, trying to pretend that he hadn't understood. His heart was pounding so hard that it hurt. He wanted to stay, but he knew that it wasn't wise. Nothing had changed, after all, just because she'd kissed him. He opened the door, but then he turned back to her.

"Can't make peace with it, Becca."

"I can see that."

"I'm sorry."

She shook her head. "I can't fault you for honesty, Dan. You obviously just don't feel the same as I, we, do."

He wanted to tell her that it wasn't so, but something had risen into his throat, and he couldn't have spoken even if it had been right to do so. Instead, he just stared at her, hoping that his emotions didn't show on his face. God knew that he wanted her, but she and her kids needed a whole man. They deserved that.

Finally he forced himself to get into the truck. Reaching up, he adjusted his mirror, more to break the connection that he felt with Becca than because it needed alteration. An image of Jemmy materialized. She was leaning across the fender of her mother's car with her arms flung out and her cheek pressed to the metal, as pathetic a picture as he'd ever seen—and quite calculated. He fixed the view and checked the side mirror. Becca was at the window, so he rolled it down, grinning at the child's dramatics and his own susceptibility to it.

"Give her ice cream," he pleaded, wrinkling his brow in supplication.

Becca smiled. "I will. After dinner. If she behaves herself."

He nodded and started the engine. Becca called to Jemmy, who dragged herself listlessly from the car and trudged toward her mother as if going to the guillotine. Becca traded a knowing look with Dan and held out a welcoming arm. He chuckled and rolled up the window. As soon as Jemmy was held safely to her mother's side, he backed the truck around her car and turned it down the road. When he glanced up into his rearview mirror again, it was to the image of Becca and those two kids standing there in the dusty yard of their little house.

It seemed all wrong somehow, but he couldn't quite figure out why. Whatever it was, it surely had nothing to do with him.

Chapter Seven

Dan made himself a tasty supper of chicken and dumplings by following a recipe e-mailed to him by his mother. It was way too much food to eat at one sitting, but that just meant that he wouldn't have to cook again for a while—and that he couldn't risk staying late at Becca's for at least a couple of days. Funny how his life had narrowed to whether or not he could safely spend time with her and the children.

Sitting at the table over his plate, he wondered if Jemmy had gotten her ice cream and knew that she most likely had. Unless she showed up her little self, her mama would have no reason not to keep her word. He hoped the imp was properly grateful. Even tonight with her put-upon face and mistreated-miss act, she'd made him want to smile.

CJ would get ice cream, too, of course, and gobble it down with all the finesse of a baby bird. By spoon or hand, it didn't make any difference to that boy. Yet even as he was cramming it in or opening his mouth in automatic demand for more, he was watching everything and everyone around him. More often that not, Dan had to admit, the boy was watching him. Who was he kidding? The light of hero worship in that child's eyes made him feel ten feet tall. But what would he see in those green eyes, so like Becca's, when he failed to respond to his cries?

Dan felt as if he had one foot nailed to the floor and couldn't go anywhere except around and around in circles. One moment he wondered if he could really belong with Becca and the kids, and the next he had to face the fact that he could not be all that they needed. He thought of Becca: her pretty, peaceful face, those wide, soft eyes, that Cupid's-bow mouth, the perfume of her—all Becca without any hint of anything artificial, just clean and feminine—her endless patience, forthrightness, her happy faith…. Why did feel as if he'd lost her when he'd never even had her? He felt so confused. For days he'd been praying about it.

Don't let my desires keep me from doing the right thing, Lord. Show me what's best and help me do it. I want to do what's best for Becca and the.kids.

Only by talking to God could he find a measure of peace that allowed him to go about his business.

Rising from the table, he cleaned up after his

meal and wandered into the living room to catch the late news. The weatherman predicted a chance of rain tomorrow. Good thing he'd gotten the roof on Becca's porch. With that thought, he took himself upstairs to bed, as weary as ever he had been in his entire life.

Dan awoke with a jerk. It was dark inside his room and as still as the grave, despite the opened window beside his bed. Still tired, he first rolled onto his side and looked at the clock on the bedside table. Three in the morning. The tingle of his nerves told him that he would sleep no more this night, and he resignedly rose to a sitting position.

His natural circadian rhythm had been disturbed for a time after his concussion. He'd essentially slept for days after the explosion, only to awaken for the first time in the middle of the night to an eerie silence, feeling his own heartbeat and breath in a way he never quite had before. For a time he'd been frightened and disoriented by the tilt and sway of his world. Then he'd realized that he was aboard a hospital ship. Some hours had passed before he'd fully understood that he could not hear a blessed thing, not even the rotor staccato of the helicopter that ferried him to an air base for transport home to the States.

After that he'd slept only fitfully for months, a combination, the doctors had said, of stress, jet lag, disorientation, worry and idleness. He'd soon discovered that no easy remedy existed, for the simple reason that he could no longer rely upon an alarm clock to tell him when to get up. An orderly had awakened him on the ship, but gradually he'd had to learn to pace himself, develop a routine, read his own body and organize his life around an uncertain beginning to his mornings.

It was his habit to lay out his clothing for the next day. He got to his feet, and without bothering with the light pulled on the jeans that he'd left folded over the foot of the bed, shrugged into the T-shirt waiting atop the dresser and picked up his boots, into which he'd poked a clean pair of socks. He carried the heavy, familiar footgear out onto the landing and down the stairs, where he went into the kitchen for a glass of milk.

He poured the milk by the light of the refrigerator and drank it all, standing, then poured another glass and fished around in the cookie jar for a couple of stale macaroons, which he carried in his teeth as he walked through the dark house to the study. Might as well catch up on his correspondence while he had a chance. E-mail had been piling up in his box. Sitting down in the comfortable leather desk chair, he laid the cookies on the blotter right next to the tall glass of milk and pulled on his socks and boots before settling down to his little feast. One cookie into it, however, he lost his enthusiasm for the second.

What was wrong with him? Even during his time

in the hospital he hadn't felt like this. Fear as real
as the chair beneath him gripped his heart, and he
began to pray with a fervency that bordered on
panic. In the midst of it he found himself remem-
bering the last verse of the forty-second Psalm.

"Why are you downcast, O my soul? Why so
disturbed within me? Put your hope in God for I
will yet praise Him, my Savior and my God."

He lifted his head. Something was wrong. The
hair rose on his forearms and the back of his neck.
His skin prickled and tightened. He felt the crack
of thunder in time to turn his head to see the flash
outside the window. In that blink of light he saw
the branches of the trees swaying wildly. A moment
ago it had been as still as death without a breeze
of any sort, but in the time it had taken him to dress
and come downstairs for a glass of milk and some
cookies, a storm had arisen. Storm. The word
whirled through his mind, followed instantly by another, much more ominous.

Tornado.

Jumping to his feet, he hurried out onto the front
porch, right to the edge of the steps, where he
paused, steadying himself with one hand on a
sturdy square column. The smell of rain filled his
head and lungs, but even as the wind died away to
a chilling breeze, lights began to come on around
town. He watched them, one by one, then caught
sight of a police vehicle at least two blocks down,
speeding toward him with flashing colored lights.

The warning siren must have sounded, which meant that a twister had actually been sighted! And as deaf as he was to the alarm, Becca and the kids would be, too. The horn was mounted atop a pole on the edge of the school grounds and could not possibly wake them from a sound sleep so far from the center of town. Rain began to pour down in sheets, as suddenly as if someone had turned on a tap. It was foolhardy to drive in such a tempest, but he couldn't take the risk that the storm would miss Becca's place.

Galvanized, he ran back into the house, taking the stairs two and three at a time as he made for his bedroom. Grabbing keys, wallet and a flashlight from the nightstand, he pelted back down the stairs and out of the house to the truck parked in the carport. He gunned the engine in Reverse all the way out into the street, then forward as fast as he could go, the rear end slewing from side to side on the rain-slicked street.

The trip out to Becca's house had never seemed longer, even as the rain began to let up. When he turned off the county road onto her sandy drive, he wondered why in the world anyone would build a house so far off the road. As he bumped over the last little rise, the truck rocked crazily, and it was then that he saw the gray funnel cloud begin to dip down out of the churning black mass overhead, and he laid on the horn. The flashing red light on his warning panel let him know that it was indeed blowing. He could only pray that they had time to get to safety.

Bailing out of the truck before the engine had even died, he crammed the flashlight into his back pocket and ran for the house. Becca met him on the porch in her nightgown and robe. The air had grown ominously still again.

''Get to the cellar!''

Eyes wide, she turned back into the house without a word, and he followed, right on her heels, straight to the kids' room. Becca went to the crib, and as Jemmy roused, Dan swept her up into his arms.

''Hang on to my neck.''

He realized that Becca was grabbing clothing, and he took it from her, bundling it into his arms with Jemmy even as he pushed Becca back into her own bedroom. He gave her two seconds to snatch up what she could for herself, then seized her by the arm and propelled her into the living room and across it to the kitchen. Shoving aside the table with one hand, he threw open the cellar door, beyond thankful that he'd installed a new one along with a sturdy set of stairs. All but tossing Becca and CJ down those steps, he dropped down behind them and let the counterweight on the door slam it shut.

For a moment he stood there at the bottom of the steps in the pitch-black darkness, pumping damp air in and out of his lungs, heart racing as he waited for the light. Then he realized that if he wanted light, he was going to have to provide it for himself. Still clutching Jemmy, who had a stranglehold on his neck, he let the clothing fall and reached into his back pocket for the flashlight, then flicked it on.

Becca stood a few feet away, jostling a screaming CJ. A trickle of sand drifted down from overhead, and Dan's skull felt as if it was being compressed slightly.

"We're okay," he said, as if to reassure himself. "We're okay."

But he sensed the maelstrom whirling overhead, and the skin prickled on his arms and legs. Jemmy was trembling, and Becca's face was ashen with fear. She looked up at the ceiling, jiggling the baby, and Dan wondered what she was hearing.

"Can you hear me?" he asked, and she lowered her gaze to his face, then gave him a nod. "Too loud?" She shook her head. Willing his heart to slow, he sucked in a deep breath through his mouth. It tasted of dirt, dampness and panic. Perhaps it was his inability to hear the storm that allowed him to calm himself. Now he had to calm the others. "Settle in. Get comfortable."

He carried Jemmy over to a wooden box about as old as he was and carefully set her atop it. Shivering, she pushed hair out of her face and looked up at him with wide, solemn eyes, trusting him to keep her safe. He took stock. Becca had stored a jumble of things down here, including some of Abby's canned peaches and pickled okra. He spied an old kerosene lantern and went to check it for fuel, slipping past Becca and the baby in the narrow confines. Calmer now but still sniffling, the boy reached for him. Dan smiled, but took care of the lantern first. Luckily, it felt heavy with sloshing liquid.

"Matches?" he asked Becca, and she reached into a corner of a dusty shelf, coming up with a small box. While he lit the lantern, she pulled out two cheap, folding lawn chairs, the type with woven plastic seats, and placed them within the circle of light. To save the batteries, Dan switched off the flashlight and placed it, lens down, on one of the shelves that lined the narrow, dusty, underground room. When he turned to Becca, she handed him CJ, then followed the boy right into Dan's arms, all soft and warm and woman. A moment later he felt Jemmy wrap herself around their legs.

"It's okay," he said against the top of Becca's head. "Safe." Had any woman ever smelled better than this one? he wondered, closing his eyes for a moment.

Thank You, God. Thank You. I know You woke me just in time.

CJ grabbed hold of his ear, but Dan wasn't ready to give up that sweet, soapy perfume just yet. Presently Becca pulled away a little, and when she wiped the tears from her cheeks he realized that she'd been crying. She turned her face up and asked, "How did you get to us in time?"

He gave her a lopsided grin. "Went fast."

She punched him lightly in the midsection. "You took a big chance driving out here in this kind of storm."

"You can't hear tornado siren."

"Neither can you."

He chuckled, feeling the tension in his chest begin to loosen. Oddly, it made him feel a little weak in the knees. "Better sit."

He pulled around one of the chairs and gingerly lowered himself into it, shifting the baby onto his knees. Jemmy had glued herself to her mother. Becca pulled the second chair close and sat down facing Dan, Jemmy on her lap. As she kept casting worried glances upward, Dan figured the storm must sound pretty fierce.

"What time is it?" she asked.

He shrugged, not having thought to grab his watch. "Half past three? Not sure."

She tilted her head. "How did you know?"

He understood perfectly well what she was asking. Leaning forward slightly, one hand steadying the boy, he told her. "Just woke up. Felt wrong. Knew it was coming here."

"Thank God," she said fervently.

"Yes. Thank God."

Jemmy suddenly jerked and cried out, clutching her mother.

"What?" he asked. Becca answered, but she was looking up, so he didn't understand. "Becca!" he said sharply, and she abruptly dropped her gaze, blinked and answered him.

"Something hit the door."

No telling what that was, but it meant something had been flying around inside the house. "Raining?"

"I think so. It's quieter now."

"Good." At least, he hoped it was good. Frankly, he wasn't too sure just how watertight this old root cellar was, but he saw no point in dwelling on that at the moment.

"I was in a typhoon once," he said—anything to distract them.

"What's a typhoon?" Jemmy wanted to know, turning her face up to him. It looked as if she'd pronounced it *tied-foon*.

"Big storm at sea," he told her.

"Were you on a ship?" Becca asked, and he nodded, answering Jem's question before she could ask it.

"Big, big boat, lots bigger than a house." Jemmy's eyes went wide. For the first time he realized that her eyes were almost the same color as his, as blue as a cloudless sky. "Wind blew hard. Ship went up and down." He rolled his arm and hand in the air, demonstrating what the troughs were like during a typhoon in the open sea. "Like a roller coaster."

"Nuh-uh!" Jemmy said skeptically. Then, "What's a roller coaster?"

Her mother explained that. Then he told them, as best he could, how they'd lashed themselves into their bunks while dishes and various gear had tumbled and crashed, rain and seawater deluging everything topside. "Scary," he said finally, realizing that he'd talked more in those minutes than he had in many months.

CJ slapped a wet hand against Dan's cheek just then, and Dan realized that his hand wasn't all that was wet. "Any diapers?" he asked.

Becca bit her lip and said, "I'll check." Shifting Jemmy off her lap, she went to the foot of the steps and gathered up the things they'd dropped earlier. "Might as well get dressed," she said, carrying them into the light. She placed the lot on the chair and plucked out several items, including a disposable diaper, which she held out to Dan. "Think you can manage CJ while I take care of me and Jemmy?"

"Try," he said uncertainly, looking at the bits of clothing as he took them into his hand. He looked up a moment later to find her waiting.

"Well, turn around," she said, making a twirling motion with her finger.

"Oh." He got up and turned the chair so that it faced the wall, CJ and his clothing tucked under one arm. He sat down again and started trying to figure out what went where.

The diaper was first, of course. Fortunately CJ lay placidly with his head upon Dan's knees while he managed it. He'd dismantled sophisticated weapons less confusing than all those folds and gathers and tabs, and it wasn't until he had the thing on that he realized it was backward.

"Again," he said with a sigh, but CJ had been patient as long as he was going to be. It became a real wrestling match, and for once Dan was glad he couldn't hear, for he was sure there was much laughing going on behind him. Nevertheless, he finally got the squirmy critter corralled and saddled. Then came the actual clothing, which turned out to be a one-piece shorts-and-shirt thing with a bewildering number of snaps. He fastened the crotch together twice before he got it right, and by then CJ was completely out of patience. Hitting a moving target at a hundred yards was nothing, Dan concluded, compared to getting a tiny sock on a busy foot. In the end, Becca came to rescue them both.

Dressed simply in faded jeans, gray T-shirt and running shoes, she wasn't wearing any socks, either. "Let's just forget about these," she said, tucking those tiny stockings into a pocket. "Anybody hungry?"

Jemmy jumped up and down, the ruffled hem of her favorite flowered nightgown belling out to reveal the cuffs of the shorts she wore underneath. Apparently Becca hadn't managed to grab her a top. At least she had snagged a pair of tennis shoes for her. As Becca reached for two jars of sliced peaches and a small box of plastic forks, Jemmy knocked into the empty chair. She stilled at once. Becca obviously chose not to scold the child in these trying circumstances, a decision Dan found wise.

"We'll have to eat out of the jar," she said, handing one to Dan. "Try not to get syrup all over yourselves. We may be wearing these clothes for a while."

She smiled, but Dan saw the worry in her gaze and nodded mutely. Becca calmly set her chair upright and parked herself in it, Jemmy coming to lean against her knee. Dan held the plastic fork in his teeth while he twisted open the jar, feeling the *pop* that told him the seal was good and the fruit safe to eat, but he hesitated before he put the fork into the jar, looking up at Becca. She seemed to know exactly what he was thinking and reached out her hand for his. He clasped her fingers and bowed his head.

"Dear Lord, thank You." It was all he could get out, but it was enough. Becca squeezed his hand and let go. When he looked up, she was forking a peach slice into Jemmy's mouth.

The best that Dan could manage with CJ was to lean the child way out over his legs and quickly slide a whole peach slice into his gaping maw. The boy could swallow almost without chewing, and half the quart jar was gone before Dan got his first bite. He ate the rest with CJ sitting quietly against his chest, drank the syrup, dropped the fork into the empty jar, which he placed out of the way on a nearby shelf, and wiped his sticky mouth with the palm of his hand. When he looked down at CJ, he saw that the boy slept. Jemmy was drinking the syrup out of the jar she'd shared with her mother.

"What do you hear?" he asked Becca.

"Nothing for some time now." The look on her face said that, much as she dreaded it, they could probably safely look outside.

"Wait for daylight," he suggested, and she nodded agreement. Neither had to say that the dark could hide unknown dangers if the storm had done much damage.

Dan didn't know how long they sat there, her cradling Jemmy, him holding a sleeping CJ, but the air had gotten close and stale and his joints felt stiff and uncomfortable when he finally rose.

Jemmy, too, came to her feet, so he slid CJ into his mother's arms and reached for the flashlight. "Let me look first."

Becca nodded, and he slid his palm against her cheek before he went to the stairs. Dread filled him, but it was easy enough to set aside. They were all alive and well. And together. He'd not ask for more than that.

He climbed the steep steps, put his shoulder to the door and shoved upward, but it barely budged. Not a good sign. He pocketed the flashlight and tried again, feeling something heavy slide around on the top of the door. He looked back down into the cellar, saying, "Becca, help me."

Becca rose and placed CJ in the seat of the chair, instructing Jemmy to stand in front of him and keep him trapped in his seat. Jemmy seemed to relish the job. Becca squeezed up the steps beside Dan and placed her hands flat on the underside of the door. He pulled her up higher.

"Use your back."

She maneuvered until she got her shoulders pressed up against the door. Dan craned his head out of the way to accommodate her. He patted her legs to let her know that she should push with those rather than just her back.

"On three." She nodded, and he counted. "One, two, three."

For a moment he didn't think they'd make it, but then whatever it was blocking the door slid free and the door literally flew open. Gray light flooded the stairwell. Dan caught Becca as she lost her balance, steadying her with his hands.

"Wait," he said, promising her with his eyes that no matter what they found, all would be well. She shrank back, and he climbed up out of the hole of the cellar into…chaos. And open air. The refrigerator had been blocking the door, but that was about the only recognizable shape he saw. Becca's house lay in jumbled piles of debris, bits of newly installed insulation fluttering like pink dandelions in the breeze. Even the floor had buckled and tilted crazily. It wasn't light enough to see much more, but what he could see was catastrophe.

He turned back to the cellar and looked down to

find Becca waiting with wide, uncertain eyes, CJ on her hip, Jemmy's hand clasped in hers. He reached down and drew her gently upward, saying, "Sorry, honey."

Tears filled her eyes, but for a long moment she looked only at him. Then she took that last step up and out. Wandering slowly forward, she clasped her son to her and took it all in. Dan let her go, let her deal with it, but when she reached the spot where her new porch had stood, now swept clean of even the sand that had once covered the hard ground, she fell forward onto her knees. Yanking Jemmy along with him, he rushed to her side and went down onto the dirt with her, pulling her into his arms, pulling Jemmy in with them, CJ wedged between their chests.

She sobbed, but the children, oddly, remained dry-eyed. With Jemmy it was shock, with CJ confusion. Dan held them all as close as he could get them and waited it out. Presently Becca began to pray. He couldn't hear what she was saying, but it didn't matter. As he held her with her face tucked into the curve of his neck, he could feel the words against his skin, and though he couldn't identify a one, he knew the essence of them, for they were the same words that his own heart prayed.

Why?

Help.

What now? How do we fix this?

We survived.

Thank You.

Chapter Eight

They sat on the ground for a long time as daylight gradually brought the devastation into full relief. Becca didn't want to look. She didn't want to leave the shelter of Dan's arms. If ever she had doubted that Dan Holden was the answer to her prayers, she would not do so again. He had saved them. God had used Dan to save her and her children.

''What do we do now?'' she asked his shoulder.

His only reply to that was to bracket her face with his hands and tilt her head back because, of course, he couldn't have heard her. She smiled wryly and saw in his bright eyes a tender concern that brought fresh tears to her own. The children began to stir.

Jemmy sat flat on the ground, leaning against both Becca and Dan, and now she rubbed her eyes as if awakening. CJ had slipped down to Dan's lap when he had shifted off his knees to sit with his legs folded back beneath him and slightly to one side. Her poor baby was holding the hem of Becca's T-shirt and the sleeve of Dan's as if he needed to be doubly sure that he was anchored to this world. He tugged uncertainly at her, and she straightened away from Dan to smile blearily at CJ and take him into the fold of one arm, wrapping the other around Jemmy.

"I don't know what to do next," she said to Dan, feeling stupid.

He got to his feet, dusting off his jeans with busy whacks of his hands as he glanced around the immediate vicinity. "Head for town."

Jemmy stood, keeping close. Dan reached down and pulled Becca to her feet by one arm, CJ sliding into position on her hip. He held her gaze for a time, as if willing her to be strong. Becca steeled herself, full of dread, then turned and caught her breath.

It was even worse than she'd first thought.

Broken, soggy bits of debris were snagged in the bushes that had grown up around the fencerow. Much of it was tangled in twists and curls of barbed wire. A cast-iron skillet and a single fork, the plastic dish drainer, the broken handle of a broom and the sides of a rattan clothes hamper were strewn about the yard. Her car lay on its side, missing its hood and most of its glass. A fence post had been embedded in one wheel well and stuck out at a

crazy angle. She saw a wooden block and a tiny
die-cast car in a clump of grass. What was left of
her television set had been buried by one corner in
the dirt next to it. The old hickory tree that stood
about fifteen yards to the east of the house was now
bald and split. Worse, Dan's truck was wrapped
around it.

"Oh, Dan," she said, turning to him.

He shrugged. "Insured."

"Well, thank heaven for that," she said, not even
wanting to think about her own situation.

Bringing his hands to his hips, he said. "Guess
we walk. Or I do."

She glanced around once more. "There's no
point in hanging around here. We'll all go."

"You sure?"

She wasn't really, but she couldn't think of anything more depressing than sitting here alone with
the kids. "If you don't mind. We'll have to take
our time."

He reached for CJ and her hand. "Plenty of
that."

She took Jemmy's hand with her free one, and
they started off at a sedate pace, Dan matching his
gait to Jemmy's. They hadn't gone very far, just a
few yards down the road toward town, when Becca
felt her spirits begin to lift. The air tasted clean,
crisp. The bright sun felt gentle. The sky had never
seemed so blue. She began to realize that the post
oaks lining the bar ditches that flanked the dirt road

were alive with fluttering movement. She squeezed Dan's hand, and he turned his head to look at her.

"Birds are singing."

He nodded and looked up, pointing with his chin. A pair of small brown wrens dipped and darted, cavorting like happy children. Becca burbled laughter, glad to be alive, and Dan's strong right arm came around her shoulders, squeezing and momentarily throwing her off stride. Then he pointed to one side.

"Rabbit."

They stopped and stayed still until Jemmy spotted the small gray hare with white tufted ears. It hopped off as soon as she began to speak to it, but she smiled, wonder in her eyes. Becca shook her head at that. Jemmy had seen rabbits before, even held and petted tame ones, but the whole world had become a gift with their survival of the storm.

A little farther on, Jemmy herself caught sight of a tortoise sticking its head up from a depression in the ground. It retreated into its shell as she ran toward it, but presently poked its head out again, beady eyes rolling. Becca stopped her from reaching for it, and Jemmy immediately put up a fuss to take it home as a friend for Buddy.

"This is a wild thing, Jem, not a pet."

Jemmy's lower lip began to tremble. Just then Dan crouched at the edge of the depression, CJ on his knee and a twig in hand. He dropped the end of the twig in front of the tortoise's head, and the critter snapped with shocking speed, yanking the twig from Dan's hand as it again retreated. Jemmy jumped back with a yelp.

"Bad turtle!" she cried.

Dan wrapped his arm around her and brought her close to his side, saying, "Reckon he's had a tough time, too. Better leave him be. Okay?"

Jemmy dashed a tear from one eye with a dusty hand. "'Kay."

He nodded and patted her arm before rising to his feet once more. They started walking again, but Jemmy's mood had soured, and she complained of being tired and bored. Becca began to hum a familiar song, and soon Jem was singing along and skipping ahead. Becca was beginning to feel fatigued herself. None of them had gotten much sleep, and the adrenaline surge of terror had abated. She wondered how long they could keep up the pace.

Sure enough, they hadn't gone quite a mile when Jemmy began to flag. Dan paused long enough to hand CJ to Becca and swing Jemmy up onto his back. A spurt of guilt shot through Becca, and she mentally castigated herself. She should've stayed at the house with the kids and waited for him to return with help—except the house no longer existed. The devastation boggled her mind. She didn't dare think about it yet. Better to concentrate on the here and now.

"You can't carry her the whole way," Becca told Dan, feeling hot and drained.

"Won't need to," he said, striding ahead, his hands behind him to support Jemmy, who had wrapped both arms and legs around him.

Dirt gave way to pavement, which made the walking easier but hotter. They trudged on, not speaking or pausing except to shift a child into a more supportable position. At the end of the second mile they stopped to rest. Becca's tongue was sticking to the roof of her mouth. Her feet felt sweaty, and CJ had started to fuss. She swept a place free of stones in the dirt at the edge of the road and sat down cross-legged, CJ in her lap. Dan and Jem did the same. Becca's forearms had started to sunburn. She wasn't as brown as Dan or even Jemmy. She shielded CJ with her body as best she could and sighed, pushing damp, scraggly hair away from her face. She must look a sight, but what could she do about it now?

She caught Dan's eye and said, "Wish someone would come along."

Dan nodded, squinting into the distance, his forearms balanced on his knees. "Me, too."

"I wish I had some chocolate milk," Jemmy announced.

"When we get to town," Becca promised. Providing it's still there, she added silently, biting her lip. Just how hard had the town been hit? she wondered. Were Abby and John Odem safe? She wished she had some way to let them know that she and the kids were okay. Dan seemed to be reading her thoughts.

"Don't worry," he said. "Be okay."

She nodded and put on a brighter face, though a real smile seemed to elude her.

They sat there until the ground got too hard for comfort. When Jemmy rose, so did Dan. He reached down for CJ, who went readily into his arms, and once more hauled up Becca, who let him, even as it occurred to her that she had come to depend on him even for small things like this. She pushed away a sense of desperation and fixed her mind on just getting to town.

Dan looked down at Jemmy. "Walk a bit?"

She nodded and moved between him and Becca. He lifted CJ onto his shoulders, clasping his hands behind the baby's back. CJ grabbed an ear and a fistful of hair. Becca took Jemmy's hand and squared her shoulders. Off they went.

That last mile seemed to stretch on and on forever. Heat radiated in silver waves off the pavement. The sun had grown harsh, mocking. Becca held tears at bay with a willing numbness. Dan had shifted CJ to his chest and instructed Jemmy to walk in the shadows that he and Becca cast as they trudged along.

They didn't pass another soul all the way into town, but as they drew closer they could see signs of damage. Trees and highline poles were down.

Shingles and leaves and bits of other matter littered the ground. Becca's concern for Abby and John Odem grew.

"Didn't set down," Dan pointed out. He didn't say, and she didn't have to be told, that a tornado didn't have to touch the ground to do a great deal of damage.

Jemmy began to complain and then to cry, and they were blocks yet from Dan's house. He looked to Becca, the first real signs of worry puckering his brow. "Can you take CJ?"

She wasn't really sure that she could, but she nodded and held out her arms. Once he was on her hip, the baby felt part of her again. Dan scooped up Jemmy and held her against his shoulder, stiff and sniffling, but before they could move forward, a black-and-white patrol car turned from behind an empty building onto the street and came toward them. Dan waved it to a stop, and Clay Parks got out, one of only two deputy police officers employed by the city. He was a compact man with a boyish face and easygoing manner.

"You folks all right?"

"Just tired," Dan said, sounding it. "Mrs. Kinder's house was destroyed. We had to walk in." He didn't offer any explanation for him being with them.

"Say, I'm sorry to hear that," Clay told her.

"Can you tell me if Abby and John Odem are okay?" Becca asked urgently.

Clay nodded, the brim of his brown felt cowboy hat rocking to and fro. "Saw Abby not two hours ago. They had some damage at the house. Otherwise they rode it out just fine. She was worried on account of not being able to reach you, with the phones being down. Power's off, too, but the chief called it in on his cell. Oughta be back on in a few hours."

"Could you take me and the kids over there?" Becca pleaded. "We're about done in."

"Drop us at my house," Dan countered.

Becca bit her lip uncertainly. "I don't know. Maybe we should go straight to Abby's."

Dan shook his head. "My house is closer."

"That might be best," Clay said. "The Holden place seems untouched. Besides, the Kinders are at the store, doing what they can there. I'll let Abby know where you are."

Becca nodded. She hadn't even thought about the store. What would they do if their only source of income had been destroyed? She couldn't make herself think of it just yet, and since Dan was already handing Jemmy down into the back seat of the police car, she let him propel the situation along, as she had been doing. He reached for CJ next and stepped back to let Becca slide in beside Jem before dropping down on the outside, CJ on his lap. As Clay turned the car around, Becca laid her head back and felt an ache spread from her feet up.

After a bit Dan asked a little loudly, "Anybody hurt?"

"Haven't heard of any fatalities or serious injuries," Clay answered. "Got some damage, all right. Lots of roofs tore off and chimneys down, few busted windows. Mostly straight-line winds and lightning, I figure."

Dan looked to Becca. She lifted her head and repeated what Clay had said. "No fatalities or serious injuries so far as they know. Lots of damaged roofs, chimneys and windows. He figures it was mostly from straight-line winds and lightning, so I guess you were right about the twister not setting down here."

Dan nodded and turned his gaze out the window. "That's good."

Clay looked into his rearview mirror, tilting his head back so he could see Becca. "You sure he's all right? Something wrong with his ears?"

Becca leaned forward. "Dan's been deaf since he was hurt in an explosion in the military."

"Is that so? I never knew. Heard he was working out at your place, though."

"He came out to warn us," she told Clay, wanting to set the record straight. "Good thing, too, because we took a direct hit. If we hadn't got to the cellar quick, we wouldn't be here now."

"Boy, that was some lucky!" Clay exclaimed.

"More than lucky, if you ask me," Becca said.

"We had to walk in because Dan's truck got wrapped around a tree."

The deputy whistled as he pulled over in front of Dan's house. "He got insurance?"

"He says so."

Dan opened the door and got out.

"What about you?" the deputy asked.

Becca grimaced. "Little bit."

"It's a complete loss, is it?"

"Except for the land."

"Can't take the land, can they?"

Might as well, Becca thought. With a sigh she started to slide across the seat, then paused, blinking back tears. Her voice shook when she asked, "Could you ask Abby to bring over diapers and clean clothes? We're always leaving stuff at her place."

Clay Parks looked over his shoulder, sympathy in his eyes. "I sure will, ma'am."

"Thanks."

She grabbed the hand Dan extended to her and stepped out of the car. Broken tree limbs littered the yard, and the shrubs were looking kind of bare. A window screen lay on the front lawn, and the gutter was down on one side. Otherwise, the place looked the same as before.

"I hafta go," Jemmy whined, climbing out of the car. Becca nodded as she took CJ from Dan, who bent at the waist and waved to Clay.

"Thanks."

"No problem."

Dan straightened and looked at Becca as the police car pulled back onto the street. "This is best," he said. "Room for Abby and John, too, if need be."

She figured they'd have to wait and see before deciding who was going to stay where, but she was just too tired to say so. "Right now what we need is a bathroom," she told him.

"Got two of those," he said. They walked slowly up the path and onto the porch, straight to the front door, which was standing slightly ajar. "Guess I didn't shut it good," he said, pushing it wide. He pointed to the stairs. "Up there."

Becca started Jemmy up the steps. Dan caught up and took CJ from her. She nodded a weary thanks and kept Jemmy climbing, though the stairs seemed to get steeper as they went. Finally they reached the landing, which opened onto a glaringly bare central hall with a window seat at the far end overlooking the backyard.

"Center door on the left," Dan said. "My bed room and second bath next. Two bedrooms on the right. Plus, garage apartment out back."

Becca knew he was really saying that he had more than enough space for her and the kids and the Kinders, too, but that was a temporary solution beyond which she could not begin to think. She concentrated on taking care of Jemmy.

The bathroom was long and narrow, with a claw-foot tub at one end beneath a small curtainless window. A gas heater stood between the tub and the toilet, with the sink placed closest to the door. Everything was white except the hardwood floor, faucets and the oval mirror above the sink—even the trash can.

''Get some towels,'' Dan said, walking across the hall to the linen closet positioned between the two extra bedrooms. As he carried the towels back to her, she saw that CJ was asleep on his shoulder.

''We'll just be a minute,'' she promised.

''Take your time.''

She helped Jemmy, then sent her out and took a turn herself. After she washed her hands and face and slurped some water as Jem had done, she felt better, and when she opened the door Dan was standing there alone.

''Abby's here,'' he explained.

Becca hurried down the stairs, Dan on her heels. Abby appeared in the wide living-room entrance, and Becca fell into her arms. Abby steered her back into the big comfortable room, where CJ slept in one corner of the sofa and Jem slumped in the other.

''Thank God you're all right,'' she was saying. ''I was so worried about you! We didn't know a thing until we woke up this morning and half the roof was off the house. We've been at the store packing ice into the freezers ever since. John reckoned it had missed you, and people were waiting when we got there, wanting batteries and nonperishables.'' She stopped and took Becca by the shoulders. ''Dan says you got hit hard.''

Becca nodded, and the tears started to come. ''It took everything, Abby, even Dan's truck. If he hadn't come to warn us...'' She trailed off and shook her head.

Abby turned to Dan. ''How on earth did you know? We slept right through it.''

''How *did* you know?'' Becca asked, stepping forward and wiping at her tears with both hands.

Dan slid his hands into his pockets and shrugged. ''Just woke up. Storm came, and I knew I had to get to you.''

Abby clapped a hand to her chest. ''Divine intervention, that's what it is.''

Dan nodded and looked at his feet. Becca covered her mouth with her hand and sat down in the nearest chair. She'd always suspected that God had a specific reason for bringing Dan Holden into her life, but it wasn't at all what she'd thought! Suddenly the future seemed even more of a puzzle to her than ever.

Okay, Lord, she prayed silently, *now what?*

''So long as everybody's alive and well, we can work everything out,'' Abby was saying. ''Logically, I guess the first thing is getting you settled.''

Dan said, ''Here. I'll move out to the garage apartment.''

''Oh, no, Dan,'' Becca protested, looking up

sharply. "We can't put you out of your own house."

"Dan's right, honey," Abby said. "We've got no place for you now. The back porch is flooded, and everything in it is ruined. Plus, a corner of the kitchen is open, and we've got to fix that first or lose it, too."

"The kids and I will rent your apartment," Becca suggested to Dan, but he shook his head.

"Too small. Not finished. Just a bedroom, really."

"Now you listen to Dan," Abby put in. "We'll figure out something else later."

"Room here for you and John," Dan said to her.

"No, no," Abby said. "We're fine where we are."

He nodded. "I'll help make repairs."

"Thank you, Dan." Abby accepted with heartfelt gratitude. "Gracious, we already owe you so much."

"Settle for a ride to Duncan," he said with a self-deprecating smile.

"You can take our car," Abby offered instantly, but he shook his head.

"It's better if someone else drives."

"Becca can. I'll stay here with the kids."

"Becca's tired," he pointed out.

Abby looked at Becca and said, "I'll take you, then." Realizing that Dan couldn't have caught that, she faced him and repeated it.

He nodded and walked over to Becca. Going down on his haunches, he laid a hand on her knee. She realized that she was letting him decide everything for her, but her brain felt dull and blank, and she could feel his certainty like a comforting blanket. Rejecting that required more strength than she could muster at the moment.

"Get comfortable," Dan said deliberately. "Abby brought diapers. Help yourself to anything you need. Kids will be hungry."

Jemmy perked up at that and struggled up onto one elbow. "Chocolate milk," she pleaded, "and cookies."

Dan rose, chuckling, and ruffled her hair. "Be back soon as I can," he said to Becca. "Rest. Eat. Use anything you want."

Becca felt close to tears again. She didn't want him to go. It suddenly felt as if she couldn't possibly cope on her own, but she knew that was just weariness and shock. She'd been on her own for nearly two years and much of the time before that. She looked up at him.

"Take care of what you need to," she said, "and don't worry about us."

He smiled and walked out into the foyer, his heavy boots clumping over the floor. Abby kissed her cheek and followed.

Becca sighed and bowed her head, leaning forward until her forehead touched her knees. *You'll take care of us,* she thought to God. *I know that.*

But still I worry. Help me not to, and keep me from doing anything foolish.

When she sat up again, Jemmy was standing at her elbow expectantly. Becca looked to CJ, who was sleeping soundly in the corner of the couch. She didn't have anywhere safer for him at the moment. She'd just have to trust that he wouldn't wake in the next few minutes.

She'd just have to trust, period, she mused, and went to raid Dan's kitchen.

Chapter Nine

John Odem wanted them to bring back as much bagged ice as they could carry. His stores were severely depleted due to the power shortage as people, like him, tried to save the contents of their refrigerators and freezers. As she aimed her ten-year-old sedan northward, Abby worried aloud about what was to become of Becca and the children, the cost of repairing their house and saving their merchandise and the plight of others hit hard by the storm. Dan didn't mind. He only caught a word or two here and there, and his thoughts were preoccupied with a swirl of plans of his own. By the time they completed the forty-some-mile trip he'd decided on a definite course of action.

He had Abby take him by the insurance office first, where he filed a report on the truck and pretended not to notice Abby telling the agent how he'd "saved" Becca and the kids. He was promised a visit by an adjuster within twenty-four hours and a check soon after. After leaving the insurance office, he and Abby drove straight to the bank, where he withdrew a sizable amount of cash. The next stop was the automobile dealership.

It didn't take long to explain what he needed and why, choose a red, midsized, double-cab, short-bed pickup truck, tell the man what he intended to pay for it—cash on delivery—order the warning system, leave a significant down payment and insist that it be ready within three days. When the sales manager pointed out that he'd have to send a man to Oklahoma City to find the necessary equipment, Dan forked over another hundred bucks as an incentive and walked out while the man was still talking. He hadn't thrown his weight around in quite a while, but he hadn't forgotten how to do it, and in some ways being deaf actually made it easier. The whole transaction took less than ninety minutes, and he had little doubt that the truck would be ready when he returned for it, and if not, he'd know why. He didn't have time to be patient or politic.

The final stop was the local discount department store. With Abby's help he picked out whole new wardrobes for Becca and the kids, about a week's worth of apparel, including dress clothes for Sunday. He bought nightgowns, shoes and a supply of baby goods, as well as a crib, high chair, car seat, diaper bag and a clever little monitor set with lights that flashed when it picked up sound. In fact, he bought two of those.

The most personal stuff he left to Abby, who put together a selection of shampoo, conditioner, brushes, combs, clips, deodorants, creams, under-clothes and such. While she was doing that, he wan-dered the toy section, entertaining himself with the amazing array of gadgets designed to teach and en-thrall a kid. He had no idea that toys had changed so much, but the old favorites wcrc still around, too, and he made sure to buy a combination of both new and familiar items, as well as half a dozen books.

His two final purchases were an inexpensive but feminine wristwatch and a Bible, a modern, fully annotated study version with a supple leather cover dyed rose-pink. He'd have liked to have her name embossed on the front, but they didn't do that there, so he settled for a flowered bookmark with ''Re-becca'' printed on it in flowing script.

Abby fussed about the amount of money he was spending, but he pretty much ignored her. When he added 150 pounds of bagged ice to the total, she flat threw a fit, and he wound up letting her cover that part herself, then doled out cash for the rest with a sense of real satisfaction. Abby shook her head and informed him that his generosity was apt to get a different reception than he imagined.

''Our Becca's a real independent little mite, you know. Comes from being the third of seven children growing up poor on an Iowa farm.''

He hadn't known that about her, and it occurred to him that he hadn't really bothered to find out. What Abby said about her objecting to him outfitting her and the kids was no doubt true, but he was willing to risk her disapproval in this case. It simply had to be done, and so far as he could see, he was the only one around who had the money to do it. She could kick up all the fuss she wanted, but in the end she'd accept his charity, for lack of a better word, because she really had no other immediate choice. Besides, he'd had more fun shopping for her and those kids than he'd had at anything in a very long time. She'd just have to swallow some of that pride. It wouldn't kill her. That much he knew from personal experience.

By the time the old car was loaded down with everything they'd purchased, it was riding pretty low, and Abby had a time holding the thing on the road, but Dan was too tired to care. He kicked back and snoozed the whole trip home, coming awake again only when they pulled to a stop in front of Kinder's Grocery. The lights inside the store meant, thankfully, that the electricity was on, and John Odem was as busy as "a June bug in August," as he put it, which according to Abby meant two months behind and fading fast. Dan helped Abby move the ice with the assistance of a wheelbarrow, then he climbed back into the car and let her drive him to his house, where they began the process of off-loading the remainder of their purchases.

The box containing the unassembled baby bed was tied to the roof of the car with nylon twine, the knots of which had tightened to the point where they would have to be cut. Dan carried in as many bright blue shopping bags as he could manage, left the lot in the foyer and went to grab a utility knife from the small box of tools that he kept in a cabinet over the washer and dryer just off the kitchen. When he returned to the foyer, Becca was there, her hands on her hips, outrage clouding her drawn face. She was wearing one of his T-shirts, which was many sizes too large for her, and a pair of his drawstring gym shorts.

As he brushed past her and hurried back outside to finish the unloading, he noticed that she was barefoot and smelled of soap and water. Obviously she had bathed. He met Abby on her way in with a clutch of bags and told her that he'd take care of the rest. Wisely choosing to leave the remainder of the sacks on the front porch, he went back to cut free the boxed crib. Becca met him on the front steps, primed for bear.

"What do you mean, Dan Holden, by taking this on yourself? You might have asked me what I—"

He put his head down and moved right past her, hauling the cumbersome box with him and trying not to notice how fetching she looked in his clothes. As he shoved his way through the small mountain of discount-store shopping bags on the floor of his foyer, he mused that not being able to hear did have some benefits, after all. No doubt she was giving vent to some choice words right now, but he didn't have to acknowledge them as he manhandled the boxed baby bed upstairs and into the front room on the right.

This room had belonged to his uncle, his father's older brother. Ted was a pipe fitter who'd spent the majority of his career working in the Middle East, socking back money for a retirement he was clearly unwilling to consider, despite being well past the age when most men hung up their welder's masks. Never having married, he seemed intent on leaving Dan and his sister a minor fortune. Dan didn't figure he'd mind having a needy little boy take up residence in his old childhood room.

Besides, it was time the room was cleared of its decades-old memorabilia and decoration. He'd hunt up some boxes tomorrow and clean out this room and the one next to it, which he intended for Jemmy. Every little girl should have her own room, he mused, or at least not have to share with her brother. In the meantime, he could make space for the crib by simply shoving aside some of the furniture. Becca could decide later what would stay and what would go. After opening the box and extracting the instructions, he figured out what tools he would need, then gathered up his patience and went back downstairs.

Becca was sitting in the living-room chair, her head in her hands. CJ was playing quietly on the floor, dressed simply in a diaper. Dan asked cautiously, "Where's Jem?"

Becca lifted her head to glare at him. "Out back playing."

"Abby?"

"She had to get back to the store."

He nodded. Time to pay the piper, then. "Want to go out front so you can yell at me?"

She cut her eyes to the side and folded her arms. Finally she shook her head. He dropped down to sit on the floor in front of her, one knee drawn up with his arm wrapped around it.

"Had to be done, Becca."

"Doesn't mean I have to like it," she said, keeping her gaze averted.

He moved his toe back and forth, trying to think what to say to that. "Could be worse."

She pushed her hands through her hair and glowered at him, saying, "Yeah, we could be charity cases with nothing more to our names than the clothes on our backs, a useless piece of land and a stock of canned peaches and pickled okra."

He dropped his gaze and said, "I can help." When he sneaked a peek at her, she was sitting forward with her forearms on her knees, mouth flattened, gaze level. She opened her mouth, but then her eyes filled, and she put her head back to keep the tears from falling. He gave her a moment, then got up so he could look down into her face.

"It's been a long, hard day," she said, mouth trembling.

He nodded. He was feeling it himself—the weakness that came with being emotionally drained. "It'll get better," he promised.

She sat up straight again, looked him in the eye and said, "Thank you."

He shrugged. "You're welcome."

She sighed. "You must feel like God's dumped us on you."

He chuckled. He actually felt as if he was finally understanding why it had all happened, why God had brought him back here, what his real purpose was. He finally understood that being deaf was next to no hardship when all things were considered, that he'd traded his hearing and a career for a *life* and that he was no less a man than before. Maybe just the opposite.

Now was not the time to say these things, though. It wasn't about him. She had been through a serious trauma. She needed time to adjust, to accept, to understand, and he needed time to work out some details and get everybody settled. The details, actually, were a good distraction.

He pulled the folded instructions from his back pocket and waved them at her, saying, "Now *I* could use some help."

She took the paper from him, glanced at CJ and said, "Okay, but what about that mess in the front hall?"

He waved a hand. "Dig out what's needed later. Leave the rest for tomorrow."

Sniffling, she nodded. "Fine."

Backing up, he said, "I'll get the tools."

"I'd better check on Jemmy," she replied, starting to rise, but he pushed her back down.

"I'll do it." He was happy to do it. Just plain happy, in fact, which didn't make a lot of sense because he really did hurt for Becca and all that she had lost. Furthermore, he knew perfectly well that more difficult days lay ahead before they could really say that they had weathered this storm, yet life suddenly felt right to him.

He found Jemmy in one of his old sport shirts, buttoned up to the neck and stuffed haphazardly into her shorts, sweeping the floor of her imaginary playhouse with a fallen tree branch. She looked up and smiled as he approached. He smiled back and instructed, "Stay inside the fence. Okay?"

She nodded and continued her play, talking and shaking a finger at some imaginary troublemaker.

Yes, he thought, giving a few more moments to her little drama, this was what life was really about, and he might never have known if left to his own devices. Like Uncle Ted, he might have awakened one day in a place far from home with the realization that his only heirs were nieces and nephews of whom he'd seen too little over the years. He understood now that he didn't want to be like Ted, and a profound sense of gratitude washed over him.

With it came the whisper of an almost forgotten Bible verse.

"In everything give thanks; for this is God's will for you in Christ Jesus."

In everything give thanks. Everything.

Even deafness, as incredible as that seemed.

Becca quickly realized that putting together a crib was a daunting process that in this case could have been a disaster. For one thing, reading instructions aloud to Dan proved less than efficient, especially when those instructions appeared to have been written by an individual with only a vague understanding of the English language. He simply couldn't watch what he was doing with his hands and the movements of her lips, too. This necessitated much study of intricate diagrams and a good deal of trial and error.

If that wasn't bad enough, CJ greatly complicated the procedure. He desperately wanted to get in on the act. Two adults down on the floor with an interesting array of wood and metal parts spread out between them looked like great fun to him. A situation tailor-made for bedlam. They spent at least half their time removing things from his reach or taking them away once he had gotten his hands on them. This naturally produced a series of infantile protests, complete with back arching and squeals of outrage.

Through it all Dan remained cheerful, patient

and—somehow—productive. Just when her own frustration or CJ's reached fever pitch, Dan did or said something to lighten the atmosphere. Once he even pretended to skewer himself with a long, thin piece of metal, reeling about the room on his knees and finally collapsing on his back with arms and legs lifted toward the ceiling and jiggling like some insane cartoon character. CJ threw himself onto Dan's belly with a shriek of delight, although a moment before he'd been screaming in demand of the dangerously long, thin metal piece, which Dan quickly passed to Becca before pitching the child into the air and catching him for a prolonged ticklefest. By the time he let the little urchin up for air, she had the rail guide firmly attached to the side of the bed and the conflict was forgotten.

As the parts disappeared into the whole, CJ began to lose interest in the process and realize that the result of the game was all about him, too. He knew a crib when he saw one, and he was ready to climb in well before it was safe to do so. Dan worked at a feverish pace then, having mastered the intricacies of the design, while Becca herself paced the floor with CJ in her arms, babbling a running dialogue on the delights of this new wonder. Once the mattress was installed, the casters locked and the side raised into place, she deposited her rambunctious son in the crib. CJ grasped the slender wooden rails and shook them with all his tiny might, as if to exert his mastery over his new abode.

It was then that Dan realized he hadn't purchased the appropriate bed linens—as if she'd ever had any.

"A regular sheet will do just fine," she told him, and then had to let him placate CJ while she folded and tucked the thing into place.

CJ went back into the crib and refused to get out until they both pretended to leave the room. Grinning at each other in the hall, they let him howl for a moment before swooping in to scoop him out of the bed once more and carry him off downstairs to the kitchen, where Jem was discovered helping herself to another glass of milk, her second since lunch. Her skill at this endeavor was clearly demonstrated by puddles of milk on the counter, table and the floor in front of the refrigerator. She had not, however, broken any glasses or turned over any chairs in the process. Becca coaxed her into entertaining her brother with a set of plastic measuring cups and other extraneous utensils while dinner was being prepared.

Dan kept a well-stocked larder, and the freezer tucked into a corner of the utility room proved to contain enough meat to feed them for months to come. The chest-type freezer seemed to have held its seal well and adequately preserved its contents, so it was just a matter of determining what could be prepared most quickly. They decided on hamburgers, though the package in Dan's pantry contained only three buns and he declared himself hungry enough to eat a whole cow. In the end he ate one burger with bun and all the fixings, another with white bread and a third patty all on its lonesome, not to mention canned pork and beans and fruit cocktail.

Afterward they loaded the dirty dishes into the automatic washer—such luxury!—and adjourned to the living room for a little television, very little, as it turned out. Jem was asleep before she fully stretched out on the rug in front of the set, and Becca herself was fading fast. Even CJ, who had napped much of the day away, seemed worn out. When Dan shut off the set and stooped to gather up Jem, Becca was only too glad to let him carry the child up the stairs.

What followed was unique in Becca's experience. Whenever Cody had been home, it had been his habit to take a few moments for himself while Becca prepared Jem and got her into bed. Later, often after Jemmy was already asleep, he would slip into the room and kiss her good-night. He even stood sometimes and watched her slumbering peacefully, a smile of fatherly pride on his face, but it had never occurred to him, apparently, to actually get her ready and tuck her in, and in all honesty it hadn't occurred to Becca to let him, perhaps because Jem was a girl and because her own father had never taken a hand with his children except in discipline. John Odem provided fine help with the children as a general rule, but even when they were around at bedtime, he was usually the first one to bed. Whatever the reason, she didn't expect Dan to help out with bedtime chores, even though they would be sleeping in his house.

It came as a shock when, after producing pj's and other necessary items from the mound of shopping bags in the foyer, he wrestled CJ into a dry diaper and shirt while she changed Jemmy. Then while she got the baby down, a more time-consuming task than normal, he calmly toted Jemmy into the bathroom and held her up to the sink so she could brush her teeth, which involved much more giggling and spitting than it should have. When Becca was finally able to slip away from CJ, she found Dan sitting on the side of a twin-size maple bed reading a book to Jemmy in such a soft voice that it was almost a whisper. Jem looked up and lifted a finger to her lips, as if to say that it would be rude to ask him to speak louder. Feeling a pang at her heart, Becca stood in the doorway, arms folded, back against the casing, and waited until he was finished. As she tucked Becca beneath the covers, she noticed a small, roughly triangular pink plastic box standing on the shelf above the bed. It was the only feminine thing in the room.

Out in the hallway Dan handed her a corresponding piece that he'd clipped to the back of his belt. "Monitor," he explained. "In case she gets scared." He shrugged. "First time sleeping alone, strange place."

Becca stared at the gizmo in her hand, watching a tiny light flash green as Jemmy coughed in the other room. He'd thought of everything. In the old house she'd heard through the wall every time one of her babies had so much as rolled over in the night, but this place was different—not just larger but more solid. She nodded, a lump in her throat, but when she looked up to thank him, he produced a second receiver, a blue one.

"CJ," he said succinctly.

She stared at him for a long moment and saw the weariness and concern around his eyes. He needed a shave, but the shadows on his jaws and chin just made the blue of his eyes look brighter and more vivid. She ached to feel his arms around her once more, but too much had happened for that now. She was too dependent on him suddenly, too much of a burden. She had dared to dream of finding love with him, of an equal and mutually beneficial relationship. For a while she had imagined that she could be his ears, his bridge to the hearing world, but this long, traumatic day had shown her he didn't really need a thing that she could provide. Just the opposite, in fact. He surely didn't need the trouble she'd brought to his doorstep.

If God had any purpose at all in bringing her into his life, it was to show him how little assistance he really needed. No, she rather feared that the need was all on her end. That, it seemed, was the story of her life, and she was purely tired of it, tired to the bone. In more ways than one. It must have shown.

"Better grab some gear," he said suddenly, moving toward his bedroom. "Shift stuff around tomorrow."

"No need for that," she told him, but his back was to her, so he couldn't know. She stood in the doorway of his room, head bowed as he packed up.

Large and spacious, the room was simply furnished with a ridiculously large bed, a single side table and a dresser and chest of drawers that matched each other but nothing else. He pulled things from both and tossed them into a small black kit bag, working quickly, then moved into the well-appointed bath to pick up his personal toiletries. She hated putting him out of his room, but it was only temporary. Tomorrow, she decided wearily, she would figure out what to do. He moved toward her, zipping the bag as he crossed the room.

"I'm sorry about this," she said, catching his eye, "but it won't be for long."

He smiled, stopping in front of her. "It's okay," he said, and then he reached around her, the bag swinging lightly against her back as he hugged her briefly. "Sleep well."

He was at the top of the stairs before she even thought to return his polite good-night, and then he was gone. She stood in the silent house, pink and blue monitors in her hands, and felt the weight of broken dreams around her.

Chapter Ten

Dan spent Saturday morning salvaging as many of his tools as he could from the wreck of his pickup truck. The toolbox had flown open at some point, but a number of the larger items were still inside. His levels were broken, the blade of a circular saw had been bent beyond redemption, but he had the tools necessary to help John Odem get a tarp over his back porch where the roof had been blown away. Clouds were building in the west when John dropped him back at the house, and he'd barely started on the late lunch Becca had prepared for him when the insurance adjuster arrived, having driven over from Lawton. Becca showed the fellow in, introduced him as Alan Hampton and insisted on fixing him a sandwich, which he accepted with a happy smile and words that Dan didn't quite catch.

"Can't very well eat in front of you," she said, sitting down across the table from Dan.

Hampton was a youngish fellow, affable and self-assured but nondescript physically. After making short work of the sandwich, he took out a long form and an ink pen and began asking questions about the storm, which either Becca or Dan answered. It went fairly smoothly. She was so good at helping him understand all that was being said that Dan doubted the young man even realized he was talking to a deaf person. Hampton would be writing and speaking at the same time, so Dan would totally miss what he was saying. Then Becca would ask something like, "Can you remember your Social Security number off the top of your head?" or "The mailing address here would be the same as the physical address, wouldn't it?"

Dan would concur or make some relevant correction, and they'd move on to the next question. One time she looked at him and said very deliberately, "You never did tell me the exact date you bought that truck or who you bought it from, either."

Dan had to grin at that one. "Don't suppose I did." He recited the date and place in Oklahoma City where he'd purchased the now wrecked truck, and the insurance adjuster wrote it all down.

When Hampton asked why Dan happened to be out that night, Becca supplied the answer. "It was a mission of mercy, pure and simple."

Grateful that she hadn't made more of it than that, Dan added simply, "Sirens can't be heard out there."

Hampton nodded his understanding and asked, "Anyone hurt?"

"No," Becca told him, looking at Dan. "Everyone's just fine."

"Can't mind a wrecked truck too much, then, can we?" he said, and Becca and Dan both agreed that they could not.

The form was filled out pretty quickly after that. Hampton thanked them both and left to go check out the damage, promising to return later with a settlement check. Dan offered to show him the way, but he felt confident that he could find the site on his own, so Dan let it be. He didn't really care whether or not the fellow knew that he was deaf, but he was coming to the conclusion that he and Becca worked well together. In fact, they seemed to fit pretty much like glove and hand.

"That went fine," he said to her as soon as they were alone.

"Should've," she answered, getting up to clear the table. "Though why they have to ask some of that stuff is beyond me."

He nodded in agreement, then softly said, "You didn't have to run interference for me."

He knew he'd gotten it wrong or that she'd taken it wrong when she stiffened. "Oh, I'm sorry."

"No, no," he protested, but she kept going.

"I didn't even think. I mean, it was sort of automatic."

"It's okay," he said quickly.

"No, really, you manage just fine on your own."

"You don't understand," he tried to say, but Jemmy skipped into the room then, announcing that CJ was awake from his nap.

"The monitor?" Dan asked, glancing around the room.

"I forgot it," Becca admitted with a grimace before going to rescue CJ from his crib.

Dan tamped down his impatience. Not only had he gotten the tone all wrong, his timing obviously left much to be desired. Pushing out a long breath, he looked to Jemmy and swirled a finger at the littered table. "Want to help?"

"I'll get it," she said, whirling away. Puzzled, he rose and brought his hands to his hips, his gaze skittering around the room. A red light was flashing on the alarm panel. Someone was at the front door. He stepped out into the hall just in time to see Jemmy swerve almost into the wall as she ran toward the foyer. Following, he came upon her talking to two women, one elderly, the other a mere teenager with dark, short hair caught up in all manner of clips and barrettes.

"They come to see you," Jem announced, looking up into his face. He looked at the two women.

"Are you Mr. Holden?" the girl asked. He nodded, and she went on. "Gram needs your help. The roof's plumb off the bathroom, and there's a leak coming out from under the house. John Odem down to Kinder's said you was the one to call on account of she hasn't got insurance, only he said we wasn't to telephone, you being deaf and all.''

Dan blinked, increasingly aware of the old woman's hands as she wrung them. Worry emanated from her squat, stooped form.

''It's gonna rain again,'' she said, and something in her face told him who she was.

''Mrs. Schumacher?''

She nodded dumbly. He looked to the girl. ''Are you Evelyn's daughter?''

''Yeah. I'm Jessica.'' He knew that Evelyn and her husband had died in a car crash when he was a junior in high school. Mr. Schumacher had been gone many years even then, dead of heart failure, it was said. These two were alone in the world. Dan sighed inwardly. He couldn't refuse to help.

''Got a car?''

''Yeah, out front.''

''Room for my tools?''

''Yeah, I guess.''

''Anything to cover the roof?''

''John Odem gave us a tarp.''

He jerked a thumb over his shoulder. ''Go get my toolbox and some rope.'' First he took Jemmy by the shoulder, looking down into her face. ''Tell your mom where I've gone, okay?'' Jem nodded. He went to get what tools he could carry.

* * *

It was wet, dirty work. He got the tarp in place just minutes after the rain began to pour, so the Schumacher women could use their bathroom, but the interior walls would have to be replaced, and the old house sagged alarmingly at one corner, where water seeped out of a broken pipe. Already drenched to the skin, he found an opening in the crawl space and slithered under the house on his belly. The break was all the way on the other side of the house, naturally, so it took some time to reach it, and about half the way was through mud. The water leak had apparently driven out some sort of critter, an opossum or skunk judging by the "nest" that Dan came across. Unfortunately the same could not be said for the spiders, but he knocked the webs out of his way and kept going.

He found the leak in a joint of pipe. That would be easy enough to fix. The bigger problem was the section of broken foundation beam that had caused the pipe to stress. The creosote-coated twelve-inch-square beam had broken off above ground level, leaving a jagged chunk of wood poking up and two others on the ground beside it. The beam had probably already been rotted, so the force of the storm had made the house sway enough to splinter it. If he could get that corner of the house up, the leak would stop pretty much of its own accord.

After crawling back the way he'd come, he had to hose himself off in the yard, even with rain falling, before he could go to the house and discuss the situation with Mrs. Schumacher. She told him that she had an upright piano sitting in that corner, so Dan took off his boots, dried himself with a towel as much as possible and crept through the crowded, untidy house to shift the furniture and move that piano. Once that Herculean job was accomplished, he borrowed the jack from the trunk of their car, found a few pieces of lumber sturdy enough to serve his purpose and set about temporarily leveling the house. In order to do so, he had to remove some of the siding around the foundation and make himself a special lever with which to work the jack. Even then it took all his body weight to coax the jack into lifting that corner of the house.

The good news was that he didn't have to crawl the full length of the house to check the leaky pipe again. All he had to do was lie in the mud under the newly exposed corner of the house and convince the flashlight to work in the rain. After drying the joint with some rags supplied by Mrs. Schumacher, he smeared it with plumber's putty and wrapped the area in duct tape. Weary and filthy, he once more knocked on the Schumacher door and told Jessica that he was ready to be taken home. This being without transportation was getting old fast. He promised to return as soon as the weather cleared to fix the roof, replace the broken foundation beam and put back the siding.

Mrs. Schumacher wept and tried to offer him

money, but he put her off, saying the job wasn't finished yet, and that he'd have to check the price of certain supplies. Upon seeing the blood drain from her face, he assured her that the job probably wouldn't cost more than a couple hundred dollars to complete and that she could pay it out a little at a time. He would not, of course, charge her for more than the supplies, and perhaps not even all of those if the cost seemed too much for her, but she didn't have to know that.

By the time he slogged up the steps to his own front door, he was craving a hot shower and a cold drink. He removed his boots on the porch, then stood dripping in the front foyer for a few moments, wondering how best to keep from creating a huge mess. Finally he decided to ask Becca for a towel. He peeked into the living room and saw that it was empty. So far as he could tell, no light was on in the kitchen. Everyone must be upstairs. He'd have to call out to her. At least he didn't have to worry about waking the baby. Oddly, he had to think how to go about shouting. It felt so strange, sucking in his breath, putting back his head and forcing the word up out of his throat.

''Bec-ca!''

For a moment he could only wonder if he'd made himself heard, but then she was there at the top of the stairs. She said something, but he couldn't quite make it out at that distance and figured he could let it go for a minute.

"Towel, please."

She turned and disappeared into the upstairs hall. Just seconds later she was on her way down to him, a pair of folded towels stacked on her arms. "You look like a drowned rat," she said, handing over the first one.

"Feel like one, too," he admitted. Smiling sheepishly, he mopped his face and moved to his chest.

She gave him an arch look, then draped a towel over his head and began rubbing briskly at his hair. Laughing, he let her tend to him. It felt good—unfamiliar but good. Finally she whipped off the towel and stood with it tossed over one arm, her hands at her waist.

"So what were you doing? Jem said two women came for you."

He nodded. "Mrs. Schumacher and her granddaughter." He briefly explained while toweling his pants legs. When he straightened again, he found Becca shaking her head.

"You can't help playing the hero, can you?"

"Huh? Just a temporary fix."

Becca folded her arms. "Who's going to do the real work?"

"Me. Can't afford to hire anyone."

Becca flapped her arms, and the towel with it. "There. You see. Abby told me you were going to do their work, too."

He shrugged. "So?"

"So you can't fix the whole world, Dan. Much as you might like to, you just can't fix the whole world." With that she dropped the towel, whirled and stomped quickly up the stairs.

Dan stood there, his mouth agape, as swamped now by confusion as he had been by mud and rain earlier. He couldn't imagine what was going on with Becca. She was a Christian woman, as generous as she could be. Surely she didn't expect less from him. It must be the stress of her situation. She hadn't wanted to go to work today and leave the children, but it seemed to Dan that they were handling their new circumstances better than she was in some ways. He'd just have to be patient with her, he supposed.

With that in mind, he draped the towel he was using around his neck, then moved forward and picked up the other one from the floor before beginning to climb the stairs. He went straight to his bedroom and across it to the bath, but the instant he stepped through the open bathroom door, he realized that Becca was already in the room. Quickly he ducked his head.

"Oops. Sorry." Before he could even back out the door, however, she had hold of him, her fingers curled around his forearm. He looked up uncertainly.

"It's for you, silly."

Frowning, he glanced around the room and saw the water running in the shower. "Oh. Thanks."

"By the time you gather up some clean clothes, it ought to be hot."

"Right. Great."

She shooed at him impatiently. "Go on. Get your things. When you're done, I'll wash what you're wearing."

Backing out into the bedroom, he said, "I can." He didn't want to put her to any trouble.

She rolled her eyes, following him. "Fine."

He turned toward the dresser, and when he turned back again, she was gone, having pulled the bedroom door closed behind her. She was in a strange mood. Dan scratched an ear, realized that he was itching all over and headed for the shower.

Becca stood at the kitchen sink, her back to the door, and gulped down tears. A maudlin feeling of helplessness enveloped her. She brushed impatiently at her damp cheeks and told herself that she was being an idiot. Of course Dan would go to help the Schumachers, just as he'd help Abby and John Odem and anyone else who needed it. Even her. She knew that she must not make the mistake of thinking that made her special. Dan was a talented, generous, caring man. Why that should make her cry, she didn't know.

She had plenty to cry about, of course. The storm had taken her home, the one place she could call her own, and she just didn't know what she was going to do. She didn't even have as much insurance on her house as Dan had on his truck. She'd never be able to rebuild with what she had coming, at least according to what her agent had told Abby, who'd notified the company of Becca's claim, since Dan didn't have a telephone. She wouldn't know for certain until the adjuster came, and she didn't know when that might be. Maybe God would work a miracle in the meantime. For now, everyone was okay.

As comfortable as Dan's house was, though, and as happy as the children seemed here, this was not their home, and she couldn't think of it as such. But she couldn't think what else to do, either. Somehow she had to find a way to provide her family with a home of their own, but she didn't have a clue how to do it. She'd just have to put her faith in God, rack her brain and be patient until He showed her the way.

Her insides still felt shaky, which was why she hadn't gone to work today. She just didn't trust herself to handle the stress right now, and Abby insisted that she and John had everything under control. Thankfully, tomorrow was a day of rest and worship. She'd feel more centered if she could just get to church, focus on something greater than her problems. Monday was soon enough to begin searching for solutions to her problems.

Meanwhile, thanks to Dan Holden she and her babies were safe. They had a roof over their heads, food to eat and clothing to wear. She was going to put these worries, these fears, behind her and simply gather her strength. God would continue to provide, and she would continue to be properly grateful, instead of wishing and hoping and making more of this situation than either Dan or God intended.

She knew how to do this, after all. She'd suffered loss and disappointment before, and she had always survived by trusting God. Feeling calmer, she squared her shoulders and went to tend her children.

When Dan emerged from the bedroom, clean, dry and freshly garbed, he was glad to find that Becca's strange mood seemed to have lifted. She smiled warmly at him as he walked into the living room, and asked what he had in mind for supper. Truth was, he hadn't had time to think of it, so he just shrugged. That was when she looked to the foyer and announced, ''There's someone at the door.''

Dan looked through the window, spotted an unfamiliar vehicle parked out front and turned back into the entry area. He opened the door to find the insurance adjuster on his porch, looking damp but satisfied.

''Come in,'' Dan invited, but Alan Hampton shook his head.

''I'll just leave this and go.'' He offered Dan a sheet of paper, saying, ''It's a total loss. Soon as the weather dries up a little, we'll send someone out to haul off the wreckage.''

Dan looked down at the form. A check was attached to the bottom. The amount was just about what he'd expected. "Thanks," he said. "Stay to supper?"

"That's kind, but no. I need to get back, and it's a long drive."

Dan nodded, folded the paper and offered his hand. "Appreciate your promptness."

"What I'm paid for," Hampton said, shaking Dan's hand. "Give my best to your wife."

Dan opened his mouth to correct that assumption, but the fellow was already turning away, and he didn't see any point in calling him back on account of a harmless error. He supposed it was a natural mistake. Thinking back, he realized that he had never properly introduced her because she had been the one to answer the door. Now that he considered it, they hadn't even actually said that it was her and the kids he'd gone out in the storm to warn. Shaking his head, he turned back into the house—and found Becca standing at the foot of the stairs. Obviously she had heard. He could think of no other reason for the ashen look of her face.

"Should've set him straight," Dan said.

Her gaze slid away. "Don't suppose it matters."

He nodded. She said something, but he didn't catch it, since she was turning toward the kitchen. He wondered for a moment if he should go after her, tell her that he hadn't bothered to correct Alan Hampton's supposition because he liked the idea of her being his wife, but he knew that it wouldn't be wise just then. She needed time to come to terms with her situation first. Jemmy appeared to ask if she could watch TV, and he went to turn on the set, reminding himself to be patient.

Chapter Eleven

Dan put a pork loin in the slow cooker early the next morning and insisted that the Kinders would take Sunday dinner at his house, since parts of Abby's kitchen were still drying out from the storm. Abby agreed on the condition that she be allowed to prepare the rest of the meal. Becca bit her lip to keep from saying that she'd been looking forward to some "normal time" at the home of her in-laws and went along with the plan, but she couldn't help feeling peevish as Dan handed her down into the back seat of Abby and John Odem's old car for the ride to church.

"He's mighty fond of that slow cooker," she grumbled.

"You say something?" Dan asked, cramming in next her. The kids' car seats took up almost all of the space, so he lifted his arm across her shoulders in order to make more room.

She shook her head, telling herself that his being deaf did have some advantages. Then she felt contrition. Losing his hearing was obviously the worst thing that had ever happened to Dan, and she wouldn't take one full moment's pleasure in it. Of course, if he hadn't suffered that loss, he wouldn't have come back here to Rain Dance to live. He'd be off making the world a safer place with the marines, and she'd never have met him, leaving her world a much more dangerous situation than she might have imagined. Funny how God worked things sometimes. She wished she knew what He was working out for her and the kids just now.

"Oh, ye of little faith," she whispered, scolding herself.

Dan lifted his hand to cup her chin and angle her face toward his. "What?" His voice was a little too loud, given their proximity and the intimate tone of it. She was sitting on one thigh, practically in his lap, and their lips were very near to touching. She dropped her eyelids, shuttering her gaze.

"Talking to myself."

He took his hand away, saying teasingly, "Better watch that."

She knew that he was telling her that he could read her lips even when her words were inaudible, and she felt a fresh stab of guilt. How could she think or speak unkindly of him when he had been so good to her? Suddenly overwhelmed by the confusion of her own emotions, she felt the prick of tears. Silently, as if attuned to her every thought and feeling, Dan brought his arm down around her and folded her close. She turned her face into the hollow of his shoulder and thought desperately, *Oh, God, please don't let me fall in love with him now*.

It hit her then that she had finally come to the root of her problem. The house was gone and, yes, that was cause for immediate concern, but what she feared most just now was that during this trying time her heart would run away with her better judgment. After all, she'd practically thrown herself at the man not long ago, and he'd made it plain that he didn't think he could or should be a father and husband. That hadn't stopped him from being a generous, caring friend, a sanctuary from the aftermath of the storm. *Hero* was not too strong a word for Dan Holden. On the other hand, *pathetic* pretty well described her at the moment.

Becca blinked away the tears, lifted her head and put as much space between them as she could manage within the cramped confines. By the time they reached the church, she felt bruised but more in control. During the service she managed to ignore Dan and concentrate on worship. It was balm to her troubled soul, and when her name was read, along with others in need after the storm, and special prayers were offered, outward calm finally began to transform into inner peace.

God had not forgotten her. Security rested always in Him, not in buildings or money or even other people. Solutions could be found for every problem. Patience and acceptance were possible; surely contentment could not be too far behind them.

After church, people stopped her to ask how they might help, but she asked only for prayer, and then was amazed to find that one petition that she hadn't even thought to offer up had already been answered. Flozelle Reed was a tall, thin widow nearing sixty who resembled a schoolmarm out of some old Western more than the banker she was, but she had been second vice president of the State Agricultural Bank for nearly twenty years. She was not a formal member of the church, but she often showed up for one reason or another. This morning her purpose seemed to be nothing less than lightening Becca's load of worries, though Becca couldn't know that at first.

"I understand your house was destroyed, Mrs. Kinder," Flozelle said, standing in the aisle in front of Becca with a patent leather handbag dangling from one thin arm.

"Yes, I'm afraid so," Becca admitted, aware of Dan at her elbow taking in every word.

"Your insurance won't cover the loss."

"I'm aware of that."

"We didn't require more coverage because the mortgage is small compared to the value of the land."

"I believe you explained that to me after my husband passed, Mrs. Reed."

Flozelle nodded with apparent satisfaction. "It is, however, more than enough to pay off your mortgage, and State Agricultural is prepared to suspend interest and payments until you receive settlement."

Becca hadn't even thought about her mortgage payments. Somehow, with the house gone, they hadn't seemed relevant any longer, but the mortgage more properly pertained to the land than the house. Now Flozelle was telling her that she wouldn't have to worry about making payments for a while. Then again, the balance due would take more than half of the expected settlement. Still, it was a generous gesture.

"Thank you, Mrs. Reed."

"You'll be receiving formal notification," the woman told her, "so do remember to have your mail forwarded."

Another matter that Becca hadn't even considered. "I'll do that, ma'am. Thank you again." She would have everything sent to Abby's.

Flozelle tilted her head, wreathed in iron-gray braids, and asked kindly, "Have you thought what you'll do now? The bank might be willing to loan you an increased amount of principal if you should choose to use your insurance settlement as a down payment on a new domicile, but it wouldn't be much more than you're carrying now, say forty thousand. That could buy a nice mobile home, though given your recent experience you might not want to go that route.''

Mobile homes, while economical, were notorious magnets for tornadoes. Ironically, Becca and Cody had actually considered one before Jemmy was born, but had decided against it for that very reason. It might be the best course for her now, though.

"I'll have to think and pray on it, ma'am, but I do appreciate you bringing it up.''

To her surprise, Flozelle reached out and patted her hand. "I'm a woman alone in the world, Mrs. Kinder. I try to be sensitive to those in my own boat.'' She swept a politely speculative gaze over Dan and turned away.

Becca breathed her first real sigh of relief since Dan had closed that cellar door on the raging storm. Never had she been so glad to have attended a church service. All the niggling doubts and worries of the past two days seemed to dwindle away, and she could only marvel.

"Good news?'' he asked, steering her toward the exit.

Very good news, she mused, nodding. Her faith had not been misplaced. God was already giving her direction, options. Thought and prayer would surely reveal the best course in due time. In the meanwhile, she had only to remember that God, not Dan Holden, would ultimately work out everything.

They joined the Kinders and the children on the

sidewalk out front and headed for the car. Jemmy begged to go by her grandparents' house to check on her turtle. Since John Odem wanted to change his clothes anyway, it was decided that he would drop off everyone else at Dan's and take Jem with him to the Kinder house. He would return as quickly as possible with a pair of more comfortable shoes for Abby and her favorite apron.

At the house, Dan escorted Abby to the kitchen and turned her loose with orders to make herself at home, then he went out back to the apartment over the garage to change into casual clothes, having moved most of his things the previous evening. Becca changed, too, and stripped CJ to his diaper and shirt. Before hurrying back downstairs, she laid out play clothes for Jem. Abby was already at a loss when Becca walked into the kitchen with CJ on her hip.

"Doesn't that boy have a good cast-iron skillet? I can't fry up a proper mess of squash in that flimsy thing." She pointed to the offending aluminum equivalent on the counter.

"We haven't been frying much," Becca said, meaning *any*. Her mother-in-law was old school when it came to cooking technique, but Becca herself preferred a healthier mode of general food preparation. "Do you want to just boil the squash, or should I go ask?"

"Do you mind running out back to ask him?

John's been talking about fried squash all week, and there's plenty in the refrigerator here."

Becca handed CJ to his grandmother, figuring she could move faster without his added weight to haul around. "I'll be right back." She moved quickly through the utility/mud room and out to the garage and then up the steep staircase that led to the apartment. She knocked on the door, realized how foolish that was and tried the knob. The door parted from the frame, and she stuck her head inside to look around.

The living area was small but adequate, with a window that looked out over the backyard. A bar had been built between the kitchen and the living room, giving the place an open feel. As of yet it didn't have a top on it, and there were no cabinets at all. She stood there pondering the significance of that until Dan came out of a short hallway that obviously led to the single bedroom and bath. He was pulling a T-shirt over his head, and as he tugged the tail down, he stopped in his tracks.

"Becca."

She pointed at the kitchen. "Where are the cabinets?"

"In the shop downstairs," he said, sucking in his already flat belly in order to tuck in his shirt. "Haven't finished them yet."

"You didn't put them in my house?"

He froze, but then he shook his head, and his

hands finished their work. Face oddly impassive, he said, "The old ones. They were in my way."

She nodded, even more aware than ever how pitiful she must seem to him. Even his uninhabited garage apartment would have nicer cabinets than her house would've had. Maybe that was for the best, all things considered. "They're kindling now."

"Candles?" he asked, face screwed up.

"Kindling," she enunciated crisply.

"They are. You're not," he pointed out.

"True."

He smiled and changed the subject. "Need something?"

"Oh. A cast-iron skillet. Abby wants to fry up some squash."

"Cabinet over the fridge. Hard to reach. I'll get it."

"You must not use it much," she observed, careful to keep her face in view as they turned to leave together.

"Not much."

"Healthier ways of cooking," she said as they went down the stairs side by side.

He nodded and added, "Good corn bread pan."

Once they reached the kitchen, he pulled down the skillet, then Abby sent him on his way, insisting that she would cook. When John Odem and Jemmy returned, they had the turtle with them, Jemmy insisting that the poor thing was lonely and scared since its "house" had been destroyed by the storm, too. To her way of thinking, it was only right that it come to live with them at Dan's now. Dan just smiled and said he'd build it a proper pen. Becca couldn't let her daughter think that this arrangement was permanent, however.

"Sweetie, you understand that we're only staying in Dan's house temporarily, don't you?"

Jem screwed up her face much as Dan had done earlier. "What's temohairly?"

"It means only for a little while," Becca explained. Jemmy's mouth took on a mulish set, so Becca made it clear. "We will not be staying here for long."

"But we don't got a house no more," Jem pointed out.

"We'll get another one," Becca assured her.

"With my own room?" Jemmy asked doubtfully, her preference for staying put obvious.

All Becca could say to that was, "We'll see," but she realized that the likelihood of providing more than she had before was slim. Still, her family would be best served by removing themselves from Dan's house as quickly as possible. Newly resolved, she promised herself that her time of grief and shock was at an end. It was time to move forward.

"Your truck's ready," Becca told Dan, hanging up the telephone in the tiny office of Kinder's Grocery. "Let's go get it."

Dan smiled. Having his own transportation again

would undoubtedly make things easier for him. He'd certainly been anxious about it, popping in and out of the store all day—between giving estimates and making critical repairs for folks hit hard by the storm—to see if the dealer had called.

His "to do" list was getting longer and longer, much of it on hold until he had the proper transportation. Becca had to bite her tongue to keep from telling him to slow down. She'd had her say on that subject Saturday, even though it really wasn't any of her business. Besides, it was undoubtedly better if they both stayed too busy to get in each other's way. She couldn't help getting a chill when she thought about him crawling around on rooftops and under old houses by himself, though. What if he should fall or become trapped? He couldn't hear if a beam was about to give way and go crashing down. She shook off the concern.

"I'll ask Abby if I can borrow her car," she told him, swinging out of the office to go in search of her mother-in-law. She returned minutes later with the keys and both kids. Abby couldn't be expected to watch the children and the store at the same time, and since Monday was a regular day off for Becca, the normal baby-sitter wasn't available.

They loaded up and set out. Dan was so anxious that he kept rubbing his hands together in anticipation. It was difficult to drive and converse, so she contented herself with an understanding smile. She hated being without wheels, too. That was something else for which she'd have to find a solution, since she'd carried only liability on her old junker.

CJ dropped off to sleep fairly quickly, it being his nap time. Jemmy amused herself with a book for a time, but then she began to whine about being bored and thirsty. Since she was in the back seat, Dan didn't realize that any problem existed, and Becca kept it that way, turning her head toward the window whenever she reasoned with or scolded her daughter.

By the time they reached the dealership, Jem was in a real sulk. Dan got out of the car, glanced into the back and bent at the waist to speak to Becca through the open door. He jerked his head toward Jemmy.

"What's wrong?"

"Nothing a soda pop won't cure," Becca assured him, and Jemmy instantly brightened.

"Sounds good," he said. "Better yet, how 'bout dinner out?"

Becca turned in her seat and looked pointedly at CJ. "We'll have two cranky kids on our hands if we wake him early."

Dan squatted in front of the open door and said, "Take Jem for soda, meet me later."

Becca glanced once more at the back seat, sorely tempted. She couldn't remember the last time she'd eaten in a real sit-down restaurant, but then she found her backbone and shook her head. "You go on. I don't want to inflict them on any unsuspecting diners. We'll just pick up something on our way home and see you back there later.''

Dan bowed his head for a moment, but then he rose. Draping an arm across the top of the car, he bent to look inside. ''Need money?''

''No! Abby cashed a check for me this morning.''

She could hear his fingers drumming against the roof of the car. Finally he straightened and closed the door. Becca knew a moment of regret, but she was determined to set aside all negative emotions and face the future with calm assurance—on her own, since that seemed to be what God intended. Certainly she could not allow herself to become any more dependent on Dan Holden. The poor man was already trapped by his own generosity and good intentions. She could not, in good conscience, add to or prolong the load he was shouldering. As soon as possible she would find a way to move her family out of his house. At a safe distance again, she felt sure that they could be friends. Until then, she was determined to be as little burden to him as circumstances would allow.

Dan looked at Becca with something akin to shock and hoped that it didn't show. Weariness pulled his exasperation close to the surface, and he struggled to subdue it before speaking.

''You want me to build two rooms onto the Kinders' house?''

Becca nodded eagerly and smoothed a sheet of

paper against the top of the kitchen table with both hands. "We've figured it all out. With their settlement and mine—or what's left of it after I pay off my mortgage—we could add two rooms to Abby and John's house. That way the kids and I would have a place to live until I sell the ranch."

"Already do."

"I mean a permanent place. Well, semipermanent."

"Why move again?"

"Why not? It isn't like we've got tons of stuff to cart around anymore. Besides, we've put you out of your own home long enough."

"No, you have not."

"Oh, you're very sweet, but this isn't a workable situation for us. Everybody wins my way. Abby and John get a bigger house without borrowing money. I can take my time selling the ranch and ought to make a nice profit eventually. Might even get a new car out of it, since I won't have to make mortgage payments. This really is best."

Maybe she was right, Dan thought. The past few days had been so busy that he hadn't had time to talk to her about the future. He'd been consumed with purchasing and hauling in supplies, making repairs and promising to make repairs. Maybe it was all for the best. Maybe he was fooling himself with the idea that he could be a proper husband and father. Becca certainly seemed no more comfortable here than she had at the beginning—less so in some ways. He had the distinct impression that she went out of her way to avoid him. Maybe she had come to understand what he didn't want to face. He felt duty bound to point out one flaw in her plan, however.

"Jem won't get her own bedroom."

"She will eventually. The wait won't kill her."

He didn't say that it was an unnecessary wait, that they could all just stay put right where they were from now on as far as he was concerned. Instead he nodded weary concession and finally said, "Can't get to it for a while."

"I know you're busy," she said, but she pecked at the paper with a fingertip. "When do you think?"

He shrugged, avoiding her gaze. "Hard to say."

Becca bit her lip. "Would you rather I tried to find someone else?"

He felt a sharp pain right in the center of his chest. "No."

"I've got money now, and I've heard there have been some builders coming around since word got out about the storm."

"They overcharge."

"One of them has to be honest."

He just looked at her, torn between hurt and anger. *Now* she would turn to somebody else? He had to find his voice and pummel it into some semblance of normalcy. "Your call, Becca," he said and left the house, straight out the back to the bare, lonely garage apartment where he'd camped for days now.

It seemed pretty clear that Becca had changed her mind about him. Either that or the old saying about familiarity breeding contempt had proven true.

He wanted to hit something. Instead he went to sit on the too-small bed with his head in his hands, finally rising to bathe and change. He couldn't sit across the table from Becca and the kids, pretending that they were going to be a real family soon. Telling himself that he owed her nothing, he got back into the truck and went in search of a lonely dinner. A drive-through was out of the question, of course, so he went into a fast-food restaurant in Waurika and picked up a chicken sandwich and fries, which he ate parked on the shore of the lake northwest of town, trying not to think of the dreams he'd been spinning since the storm.

The house was dark when he returned. He climbed the stairs to the garage apartment, pulled off his boots and fell into bed otherwise fully clothed, sick at heart. The next morning, Friday, he left without looking in on Becca and the kids. Nor did he stop in the house that evening or the next. Instead he worked, daylight to dark, ate elsewhere and generally kept himself busy and apart. It was the loneliest time of his life. The silence had never been so empty.

Chapter Twelve

Dan backed the long truck out of the garage and down the driveway to the street, where he parked it and got out again. He'd been debating with himself all morning whether or not he should offer Becca and the kids a ride to church. John Odem might well be on his way over here to pick them up, or she might be planning to walk. It was only a few blocks, after all, but the weather had warmed up considerably, and without a stroller, Becca would have to carry CJ. Having had some experience at that, Dan didn't think it a wise choice. So he found himself climbing the steps to his own porch and knocking on his own door like some stranger.

Jem opened the door, wearing the same dress she'd worn the previous Sunday, but this time her mother had caught up her fine, pale hair into a neat ponytail and tied it with a scarf in a big floppy bow. He recognized the scarf as one that Abby often wore. To his gratification, Jem's face lit up. She hurled herself at him, throwing both arms around his legs. He could feel her talking and felt a pang because she'd forgotten already that he couldn't hear. He gave her a rub between her shoulders, something more than a pat, less than a hug, and then gently set her back, turning her little face up in one hand. Mercy, she looked so like Becca.

''Where's your mama?''

She turned and pointed up the stairs, speaking again, and then she ran up them as fast as her little legs would carry her. Dan stayed where he was, no longer feeling comfortable in his own house. After a few minutes Jem appeared again, this time with the diaper bag in tow. A second later Becca stepped into view, CJ on her hip. About halfway down the stairs she looked up, one hand on the railing, and said, ''I didn't think to tell Abby to come for us.''

Jemmy jumped the last few steps and landed at his feet in a flurry of skirts and thumping diaper bag. He reached down for the bag, and Jem came right up into his hands herself. Swinging her up into his arms seemed the only reasonable thing to do. How slight she felt, settling against him.

Becca stepped down into the foyer and looked up at him. ''Haven't seen much of you lately. I was afraid we'd have to walk.''

He cleared his throat and tried to modulate his

tone. He hadn't spoken much in the past few days. "Been busy."

Her brow furrowed. "I see."

He stepped aside and let Becca open the door. As he followed her across the porch and down the steps, Jem laid her little cheek against his and wound her arm tightly about his neck and throat. He felt his heart cracking open.

"What's Dan doing back there?" Abby whispered, and Becca turned her head to find him parked in his old place on the back pew.

She wanted to cry. He had pulled so far back from them that at times he seemed like little more than a memory. She really hadn't even expected him to offer them a ride to church this morning, but he was too thoughtful not to. He'd drawn some pretty firm boundaries lately, nonetheless. It seemed that he was taking back his life from the Kinder clan, and she certainly couldn't blame him for that. God knew that he'd gone more than the extra mile for them already.

He'd helped Jem down out of the big, four-door truck, but as they'd walked toward the church building he had fallen behind, once more separating himself from them. Jem didn't understand. That had become obvious over the past few days, and Becca couldn't find a way to explain it to her except to say that Dan was used to being by himself most of the time. Becca did understand, but it still made her want to cry.

She looked at Abby and said, "Maybe he's more comfortable in the back."

"I want to sit in back," Jemmy complained.

"You're a Kinder," Becca said softly but firmly. "This is where the Kinders sit. Now, hush up. Service is starting."

Jemmy folded her arms mutinously, but she kept quiet until after the service. "Dan's leaving," she pointed out stridently as they crowded into the aisle. "I wanna go with Dan." Thankfully his back was turned and he couldn't hear, or rather, see her.

"Dan's busy," Becca told her. "He has things to do today. We're going to Grandma and Grandpa's and stay out of his hair."

Jem started a whine, but Becca didn't scold her. She knew just how Jem felt.

They drove home with Abby and John Odem. The Kinder house had never seemed so small and cramped to Becca before, especially in the kitchen when Abby asked if something had "gone wrong" between her and Dan.

"Of course not," she answered briskly. "Dan's a good, good friend, and he has a right to his space. He's used to being alone, you know, and this has been a really busy time for him."

Abby nodded her understanding at that, but Becca saw a flicker of disappointment in her eyes. She would not let Abby see her own.

Dan knew something was wrong when he saw that Abby was still in her bathrobe. The sedan pulling up in front of the house on a Tuesday morning was not an unusual sight, really, but seeing Abby get out from behind the wheel in a bathrobe and fuzzy slippers was a definite tip-off that this was not a routine visit. Dan braked the truck to a halt short of the street and put the transmission in Park. He drummed his fingers on the steering wheel for a moment, debating the wisdom of getting involved. In the end he closed his eyes and asked God what he should do. Then he killed the engine, got out of the truck and walked up to the front door.

This time he didn't knock; he just opened up and strode into the foyer. Becca sat on the stairs, her head in her hands. Abby stood at the bottom, one arm folded across her middle, the other hand cupping her chin.

"What's wrong?"

Becca looked up, and Abby turned. She spread both hands in a gesture of helplessness. "Stella's son came by the house early this morning to let us know that she had a stroke last night."

Dan couldn't be sure of the name. Names were always difficult. "Stella?"

Abby nodded, and her gaze traveled to Becca, whom he belatedly realized was speaking. He caught the last words.

"Around the corner from Abby, and she's my baby-sitter."

He digested that. "Stella lives around the corner from Abby." Becca nodded. "She's your baby-sitter." Another nod. He looked at Abby. "How is she?"

Abby pressed her hands together. "They think she'll be okay, but it's going to take time, and she's past seventy, so even if she eventually comes home again, she probably won't be able to see to the kids."

Becca rose. "I'll just have to take them to the store with me. We were planning on it eventually, anyway."

Abby said something to her, remembered that she was excluding him and turned to repeat herself. "We don't have anything ready. How are we going to corral them? John always intended to put together a play space for them, but there hasn't been time." She looked to Becca, saying, "You'll just have to stay home, sugar, today at least." Becca nodded miserably, and Abby added, "Now, don't you worry. We'll manage without you, and your salary will be the same."

"I can't let you do that," Becca protested. "You can't pay me for work I don't do."

"You need the salary," Abby argued.

Dan missed the first part of Becca's reply. "Until I find someone else to watch over the kids," she went on. "I'm more worried about you and John carrying the full load without me."

"I can do it." Dan didn't even realize that he'd

spoken aloud until they both looked at him with something akin to shock on their faces. For an instant he desperately wished that he could take the words back, but then he realized that it was the only sensible solution. He could take care of the kids; he knew he could. "The monitors," he said, as if that explained everything, and to his mind it did. He could clip one to each of their shirts and carry the others himself. That way he'd know if Jem was calling out to him or if the baby had awakened from a nap. He could manage, surely.

"Don't you have a job going somewhere?" Abby asked.

He shrugged. "Put it off a day or two." Becca seemed to be mulling it over. "I can, Becca," he insisted in what he hoped was a soft, sincere tone.

She flipped a hand dismissively. "Oh, I know that." Her brow wrinkled. "I just hate to take advantage of you, Dan—I mean, more than I already have." She tossed up her hands in a gesture of helplessness. "Seems like no matter how hard I try to stand on my own, I just wind up leaning on you."

"I don't mind," he said, feeling something warm spread inside his chest. Becca dropped her gaze, but she was smiling wanly. He realized Abby was speaking.

"A temporary solution, anyhow."

"Will you call Claude Benton?" he asked her. He looked at Becca and added, "Roof's in the dry so it won't leak. It'll wait." Becca nodded her understanding. He jerked his chin toward the door, saying, ''Put away the truck.'' He'd started to turn for the door when something else occurred to him. ''Jessie Schumacher,'' he said. Jessie would be a good baby-sitter for the summer, part-time, anyway. He'd been around her enough to know that she was responsible and caring. ''Good girl,'' he told Becca, ''despite…'' He swirled a finger around his head. Becca chuckled.

''They all wear their hair like that now.''

He shrugged, smiling just because she'd laughed.

''I'll give her a call, see if we can work something out.''

''Here,'' he said, pointing at the floor. ''Not there.''

''That would be best,'' Abby agreed. ''Old lady Schumacher still has everything she's ever owned. I mean, every cereal box, and it's all right there in her little house.''

''Pretty much,'' he agreed, smiling. The old gal was eccentric, but she was a dear. Still, he wouldn't want to think about Jem and CJ careening around her tiny, crammed place. Here they'd have room to play. Becca was looking concerned, so he said, ''Jess can't do it, we'll find someone else.''

She nodded at that and he went out, feeling better than he had in a while, though it probably wasn't acceptable for him to find pleasure in her difficulty. Still, it was nice to be needed. It was especially nice to be needed by Becca and her kids.

* * *

Jem slipped off the edge of her chair to her feet, abandoning the peanut butter and jelly sandwich that he'd just trimmed for the second time. He brought his hands to his hips, about to ask what she thought she was doing now, but before he could form the first word she was out the door and off down the central hall. Exasperated, he started after her.

It had been an eventful morning, with Jem spilling her cereal on her feet and him repeatedly waking the baby, first by accidentally bumping into the wall that CJ's room shared with Jem's while he was helping her change her soggy shoes and socks, and then by closing the door too loudly after putting the little character down for a nap. In the interim CJ had been fussy and demanding, so much so that Jemmy had once stood in front of Dan with her hands over her ears as he'd cradled the howling baby and announced, "You're lucky you can't hear!"

He watched now as she swerved toward the wall, brushing it with her sleeve, and headed on toward the door. Must have company, he mused, recalling that he'd seen her perform that particular veering maneuver before and always right about the same place. Curious. He hurried down the hall to the foyer, getting there just as Jem pulled open the door. She did a little hop, and John Odem swung

her up into his arms as he stepped over the
threshold.

"What's this here?" he asked, flicking a finger
at the pink monitor clipped to the front of her shirt.
It was a little heavy, but Dan was going to look
into getting her a belt.

Whatever she said in reply to John Odem's question made John smile, but then most things did. He
winked at Dan.

"Belled the cat, eh?"

"Sort of."

John nodded and said, "Thought I'd better check
on y'all. Need anything?"

Dan glanced at the blue receiver clipped to his
waistband, relieved to see the tiny light on top
blinking green, and shook his head. "Learning se-
crets of pb and j."

"Ah." John Odem poked a finger into Jemmy's
ribs knowingly. "Gotta trim every speck of brown
crust off and slice it diagonally so it makes two
equal triangles."

"She measures," Dan confirmed, lifting an eyebrow at Jemmy, who giggled and spoke to John
Odem. He glanced at Dan in surprise.

"Buddy the turtle has a rabbit?"

Dan grinned. "Found it in his pen this morning."

"Eating clovers," Jem confirmed.

"Set it loose," Dan said significantly, and
Jemmy nodded importantly.

"You can't get pet rabbits from wild. You got to

buy them, so we're gonna get one from Duncan, aren't we, Dan?''

"If Mama says okay."

John Odem sent him a doubtful look about that, but Dan just shrugged. He'd had to do some fast talking at the time. Besides, he didn't figure Becca had *all* the say. He could keep a pet if he wanted to, which he'd have to do if she absolutely put her foot down about it. In the meantime, Jem would be happy with a furry little bunny to nuzzle. He could see it now, soft and white, with a tiny pink nose. He was counting heavily on the cute factor to win Becca over.

John Odem looked at Jem. "Say, aren't you supposed to be eating a peanut butter and jelly sandwich?"

Dan realized then that John Odem hadn't stopped by just to check on them. He obviously had something on his mind, something he didn't want to say in front of his granddaughter. Dan felt a moment's unease, but he said nothing as John set Jemmy on her feet and she ran back down the hallway toward the kitchen. When she came to that spot, she swerved again.

"What's that?" he asked John Odem. "A kid thing, some game?"

"Naw, she's just avoiding the squeak."

"Squeak?"

"In the floor."

Dan brought his hands to his hips again. "There's a squeak in my floor?"

John chuckled. "Loud one."

"Where?"

They walked forward, Dan going first, until they came to the place where Jem always veered close to the wall. He stepped aside, and John Odem moved past him to demonstrate. He set one foot dead center of the hardwood floor and rocked forward, putting his weight on it. Dan motioned him aside and placed his own foot right where John's had been. As he shifted his weight onto it, he felt a pronounced give in the planking.

"Better get under there," he said, figuring that a foundation support had given way.

John Odem shivered. "Better you than me. I don't like close spaces." He grinned when he said it, but that was John Odem Kinder's natural expression, so Dan figured he meant what he'd said.

"Want to sit?"

"Good idea. Let's try the living room."

Dan followed this time, and as John Odem made himself comfortable on the couch, he took a seat across from him in the recliner. "What's on your mind?"

John smiled. "To the point. Okay. Well, then, Becca and Abby've been talking up this building-on thing, and I'm wondering how you feel about that."

Dan looked down, flicking his fingertip against

an imaginary speck of lint on his jeaned thigh. "Be a while before I could get started."

When he looked up again, John Odem was sitting forward, his forearms resting on his knees. "That's not what I mean, Dan. Fact is, I figure you're wanting to keep her."

"I want to marry her," Dan corrected, not much liking the way John had phrased that.

Only when John reared back did Dan remember that old saw about letting cats out of bags. Now, what had possessed him to blurt that out?

For a moment John just stared at him, and Dan imagined all that could be going through his head. He wasn't a "whole" man. He would never be a model father—the way he kept waking the baby and other things proved that. Just that morning he'd handed over a bowl of milk and cereal to a four-year-old without so much as a warning to be careful. No wonder she'd spilled it all over her feet. He couldn't even find a squeak in his own floor without help! No, he would never be anyone's idea of the perfect family man, not even that of an easygoing jokester like John Odem. Dan figured he was in for some straight talk—not that John could say anything to him that he hadn't already said to himself at one time or another. Still, he owed the older man the courtesy of hearing him out. He girded himself for an unpleasant dose of reality, but the last thing he expected, though perhaps he should have, was for John Odem to slap his thigh and go off into gales of laughter just before hopping to his feet and breaking into a jig.

"Hoo, boy!" John said, stabbing a finger at him. "I knew it! I knew it!" He lunged forward, grabbed Dan's hand and began pumping it enthusiastically. "I told Abby. I told her, but she said Becca said you wasn't interested." He flapped his lips at that, making Dan blink.

Wasn't interested? He shifted forward in his seat. "She is the one not interested," he enunciated carefully.

John seemed surprised, then genuinely skeptical. "Naw, that can't be right." He stroked his chin thoughtfully for a moment, then he shook his head. "No, it ain't that." He sat back down and shook a finger at Dan, saying, "That gal, she's had her eye on you since the day you showed up around here again, not that she was on the lookout, mind, 'cause she's not that sort."

Dan disciplined a smile. "I know."

"She's interested," John assured him with a nod. "What makes you think she's not?"

Dan shrugged and rubbed his palms down his thighs. He glanced casually at the monitors affixed to his waistband, very aware that his heart was racing. "She doesn't like leaning on me."

"She don't like leaning on me, neither, but I tell her that's what family's for."

"Not family."

"But you want to be."

Dan looked down again, uneasy revealing so much of himself. Finally he just nodded, but then he had to face John. "Thought once..." He shrugged. "Yes."

"You haven't said anything to her, have you?" John Odem surmised.

"No."

"Don't you think you oughta?"

Dan looked him in the eye. "Do you?"

"Sure do."

Dan noticed he was breathing a little more deeply. "You approve?"

"Of course I approve." His eyes clouded, and his customary cheer bled from his face. "I'm not saying it's an easy thing, my boy being gone, but there's the fact. It's about Becca and the kids now, and that little gal shouldn't be alone."

"Not alone," Dan said softly, wanting John to understand that he knew and appreciated how much a part of her life he and Abby were.

John Odem flapped a hand dismissively. "Abby and me, we're not gonna live forever, son, not in this world. We always knew God would have someone else for her, and we been praying for you even before we knew it was you, just as we prayed for Becca from the time Cody was a little lump till the day he brought her home to us."

Dan smiled, truly moved. "Thank you, John."

"Thank you," John said, getting to his feet again. Dan did likewise as John Odem glanced around him. "This is a good situation for her, for all of you. She'll see that, too. Soon as you ask her, it'll all come clear."

Dan gulped. "Just ask, then?"

John shrugged, chuckling. "Course, boy—no other way I know of."

Dan shifted his feet. "Shouldn't I ask her father first, maybe?"

John shook his head. "Naw, I wouldn't think so. Becca's the third of eight kids, you know, and the Stoddards seem to figure she's not much concern of theirs no more. Oh, I'm not saying they aren't good people. You can just look at Becca and see they've done some things right, but there didn't never seem to be no question of her moving back into the family fold after Cody passed. 'Sides, I doubt Becca herself would cotton to it, her being a grown woman and a mother and all. I'd just get the question past my teeth if I was you, and leave the rest to Him that knows best." He pointed at the ceiling as he said that, and Dan nodded.

Getting the question past his teeth, as John Odem put it, seemed a daunting endeavor just then, but he was glad to know that John approved of the match.

"Glad you came," he said to John, shaking the older man's hand.

"Me, too," John replied, waggling his eyebrows. "Got out of cleaning the fryer."

Dan laughed, and John took his leave, calling a farewell to Jem, who shouted something in reply, according to the flashing red light on the monitor. An instant later CJ's flashed red, too. Dan sighed, shook his head and called out for her to stay put while he went after the baby. He'd grab a diaper and change the caterwauler downstairs, then he'd open a jar of something to feed the little chunk and try not to doubt the wisdom of John Odem's advice—or think too much about what Becca might say.

Chapter Thirteen

Jemmy pinched her finger in the pantry door, causing a large blood blister to rise on the pad of it. She ran into the living room, slinging it wildly and bawling. Dan calmed her, looked it over and walked her back into the kitchen for a piece of ice, which was the only way he could think of to ease the sting. He'd barely applied the ice when she gasped, jerked toward the door and pointed toward the living room.

"What's that noise?"

He looked down at the monitor. The little light was rapidly flaring red. Dropping the ice in the sink, he rushed back to the living room. CJ was sitting inside the fireplace with the folding brass screen on its side in front of him, howling like a banshee. Horrified, Dan rushed forward and snatched him up, examining him for injuries, beginning with his head. Thankfully, he didn't find so much as a red mark on the boy, but when he glanced at his own hand he found that it was black with soot. Groaning, he looked for something to wipe his hand on, found nothing and decided to check CJ's back, which was black from his thighs to the crown of his head.

Dan closed his eyes, wondering what else could go wrong, which was exactly when CJ threw up all over his chest. Dan jumped back, holding the baby at arm's length, and stared down at himself, stunned. For a moment he couldn't think, let alone move, then he realized that a lot of bathing was going to be involved with this, and for a moment he thought he might cry. He looked at Jem, holding aloft her bloodied finger, and wondered if he was cut out for fatherhood, after all.

She scratched the back of her leg with the front of the opposite foot and calmly said, "He does that sometimes when he cries a lot."

Dan lifted his eyebrows. "Cried a lot today."

She nodded solemnly in agreement.

Dan sighed. "Got to clean up. You be all right?"

She shrugged. "Sure."

"Just sit here, watch cartoons," he instructed.

"Okay," she said, "but I'm hungry and I want a snack."

He made a face, painfully aware that he reeked. "Almost dinnertime." How could she even think about food right now?

She made a huge show of sighing, plopping down on the floor and slumping forward dejectedly.

"Don't open the door for anyone you don't know," he warned firmly.

She nodded and pressed a hand to her belly as if suffering hunger pangs. Dan rolled his eyes as he headed for the door, CJ dangling from his hands. He was sucking his fist contentedly as if throwing up had solved everything. Dan climbed the stairs and headed straight for the master bath, where he deposited the child in the deep claw-foot tub and quickly stripped off his shirt, turning it wrong side out. It was black everywhere he'd touched it. Very gingerly he removed the monitor receivers from his waistband and laid them on a shelf. Then he knelt and stripped CJ.

Quickly, one hand on the baby at all times, he ran water until it heated, then plugged the tub and let a few inches gather. Using plain old hand soap, which was the only thing he could reach, he scrubbed the kid head to toe, being extremely careful not to get any in the baby's eyes. Then he simply laid him back in the water to rinse away the suds. In the process, he cleaned his hands. He scrubbed his chest with a soapy washcloth, then rinsed it the same way and snagged a towel off the bar behind him to dry off. CJ was trying to sit up by then, but succeeded only in flopping over onto his belly and sliding around, which he found extremely funny.

He was slippery as an eel, but Dan finally managed to get him wrapped in the towel and into his arms. He tossed his shirt and CJ's into the tub, then carried the boy into his bedroom to diaper and dress him. Leaving CJ in his crib, he went back to rinse out their clothing, retrieve the monitors and dig a fresh shirt out of his dresser. When he returned for CJ, the boy was standing in the crib shaking the side rail like a monkey in a cage. Dan laughed, and CJ beamed at him, reaching up with both arms. Maybe he was right the first time and he could do this, after all.

Clean and dry, he carried the boy down the stairs, wondering if he shouldn't rustle up something for Jemmy to eat. It really was getting close to dinnertime, but she was a growing girl, after all. He walked into the living room, musing that he needed to get a fixed screen for that fireplace if he could find one at this time of year, and opened his mouth to ask Jem how she felt about an apple. His blood ran cold when he saw a strange man sitting on his couch.

"Jem!"

She popped up from the chair, snagging his attention. "Danny," she began. At least, he thought she was calling him Danny; at the moment he was both too relieved and too angry to care.

"I told you, don't open the door!"

She blinked and shrank back. "But I know Mr. Dixon."

Dan shifted CJ to his hip, aware that his heart was still beating at double time. It was true that he'd told her not to open the door *for anyone she didn't know,* but he'd meant her mother or grandparents. Seeing her stricken face now, he swallowed and turned to the stranger.

"Dixon?"

The man rose to his full height. He was a large, bluff, handsome man somewhere in his fifties, a rancher by the look of him and the pale straw cowboy hat resting on its crown on the sofa cushion. He put out his hand, pale gray eyes twinkling. "Call me Frank," he said.

"Dan Holden." They shook hands briefly. To Dan's surprise, CJ reached for the other man.

Frank Dixon patted the boy on the head, winked at Jemmy and said, "We're old friends. I'm Becca's neighbor. Own the section to the north of her place."

Dan frowned, still not sure what to make of a fellow who would just waltz into another man's house and make himself to home. "Uh-huh."

Frank Dixon hooked his thumbs in his belt and said, "I'm sure sorry about the storm. Broke my heart when I stopped by there and saw nothing but the foundation of the house still standing. Sure wiped her out."

Dan nodded. "Yes."

"Thank God she and the children made it through unscathed." He shook his head. "It's a pity what that little gal's been through. Anything I can do for her? Anything at all? I saw the car was mangled. I could loan her one of my trucks. Wouldn't be any bother."

"Nice of you."

"I'd sure do that and more for sweet Becca."

Dan frowned. The use of another vehicle would be convenient, and he had no right to turn down the offer on Becca's behalf, but he couldn't quite stomach the idea of Dixon stepping in at the eleventh hour, so to speak.

"We're getting by just fine for now."

"Good. That's good." Dixon rocked back on his heels, lips pursed. "I was told that she might be interested in selling her acreage. Thought I might sound you out about it."

Dan felt his heart thump in his chest. Seemed as if Dixon thought Dan might have more claim on Becca than he really did, and here was his chance to foster that idea, but he couldn't take it that far. "Becca's land," he finally said. "Speak to her."

"I see." He looked down at his toes, and Dan missed what he said next. He tapped the big man on the shoulder. When he looked up, Dan motioned with his hand that he would have to speak face-to-face. Before he could say that, however, Jemmy stepped close to his side, wrapped her arm around his leg and spoke. Dan knew by the expression on Dixon's face that she was telling him about his deafness. Dixon looked up quickly. "Sorry. I didn't know."

"It's all right. I read lips."

"Very well, apparently."

"Well enough."

Frank Dixon smiled. "You wouldn't remember me, but I knew your daddy when he was principal out at Jefferson Elementary."

"Not surprised."

The big cowboy rocked back on his heels. "I suppose Becca's down at the store?"

Dan glanced at the clock on the mantel. "Might be."

Dixon pursed his lips. "Would you tell her I came by? I hate to see her sell up after all she's done to hang on, but I'd give her a fair price."

Dan made a quick decision. Frank Dixon struck him as a friendly, well-meaning—if a little too familiar—fellow, and Becca was wanting to sell. He tried not to weigh his own personal interests against that. "Sit, wait a spell. Could be on her way home now."

The big man smiled. "Don't mind if I do." He lowered himself onto the couch once more.

Dan took the chair that Jem had vacated, aware that he owed her an apology. He hadn't meant to shout at her, and the whole thing was his own fault, but she had to know that it wasn't safe to open the door without him or another adult present, not even in Rain Dance. They could have that talk later. He

might as well start mending his fences in the meantime, he figured, so he looked at Jem and patted his
knee. She happily scrambled up to his lap next to
CJ, and he gave her an affectionate squeeze. They
traded a smile before he turned back to their company.

"So, Frank," he said, "you a rancher?"

Dixon nodded and launched into a recitation of
the stock he was raising. He was still talking about
Angus crossbreeds when Jem alerted Dan to
Becca's presence. She came into the room carrying
grocery sacks and saying, "I brought home supper." But then she stopped in her tracks. "Frank."

The sacks were quickly deposited on the end table, and in short order she and Frank Dixon were
hugging each other. Dan felt his heart drop like a
stone. Apparently Dixon was plenty familiar. Even
when Becca broke away, she was still smiling at
and talking to Dixon.

All Dan caught was, "So good to see you." Then
she turned to the children.

Jemmy jumped off his lap and threw herself into
her mother's arms. After hugging her, Becca swept
up CJ and kissed him, still talking to Dixon. She
never even spoke to Dan. In fact, she turned her
back on him in order to continue speaking to Frank
Dixon.

Face and throat burning, he got up and made
himself scarce, gathering in the grocery bags and
carrying them into the kitchen. So much for getting

that certain question past his teeth. At the moment his teeth were clamped so tightly that he couldn't have gotten a whisper through them.

It was a double-edged sword, Becca thought. On one hand, it cut through all her problems. With the money Frank was willing to pay her for her quarter section of land, she could replace her car and get about making a home for herself and her children. On the other hand, it meant the end of dreams— first that which she and Cody had struggled so hard to fulfill and also the one she had been so tempted to believe in since she'd first asked Dan Holden for his help. Perhaps that was as it should be. A dream without God's will in it was as insubstantial as a puff of smoke and about as worthwhile. Still, she wouldn't be human if she didn't feel some trepidation and disappointment. She had some suspicions about Frank's sincerity.

She put that aside as best she could, reasoning that this was proof of God's intention. Why, only that morning John Odem had warned her that it could take months, years even, to find a buyer for her property. Yet that very afternoon Frank had walked in with a generous offer. She really should have called the Dixons right after the storm. Instead she'd sat around feeling sorry for herself and making Dan feel responsible for rescuing her.

Poor Dan.

CJ on her hip, she walked into the kitchen. While

she'd talked with Frank, Dan had put away the groceries, set out the carry-in and gotten down plates.

"Sounds like you've had a hard day," she said. Then she shook her head and waited patiently for him to look up and notice her.

"Your friend gone?"

Dan's voice was strangely stilted and without inflection sometimes, but at others it sounded raw with emotion. She figured the emotion that she was hearing now had to do with the day he'd had rather than with Frank, but she was happy enough to discuss the latter.

"I should have thought to call Frank and Iola."

"What?"

She said it again slowly. His face puckered up.

"I-o-la?"

"Iola Dixon, Frank's wife."

Dan's face went oddly blank. "Married, is he?"

"Well, sure. Their son and Cody were best friends. I think Frank is the one who put cowboying into Cody's head."

"That a fact?"

"Um-hm. The Dixons have always been good to us. He bought all my stock after Cody's death, and he doesn't even raise horses. He's always sworn he sold them at profit, though."

"Now he's offering to buy your land."

She nodded. "I can't help wondering if he really needs the land or if he's just being nice." She shifted CJ on her hip. "He says he's thinking about building a feedlot."

For a long moment Dan said nothing, then, "Could bring in jobs."

"Hadn't thought of that." She bit her lip. If Frank was serious, she wouldn't be the only one to profit from his generosity.

"So?" Dan asked.

"Am I going to take his offer? Most likely. Unless…" She shrugged.

"Don't like being rescued," he concluded.

"It's not that," she told him honestly. "I just don't want to take advantage."

He smiled and shook his head, advising, "No rush. Pray on it."

"Yes, I'll do that."

He nodded at the containers in the center of the table. "Smells good."

"Barbecue," she told him, "and we better get to eating it."

She turned to call Jemmy, and he pulled the tray off the high chair for CJ. In half a minute they were seated around the table and filling their plates. They talked over the meal about the day he'd had. She couldn't help smiling sympathetically when he told her about CJ. She'd already had the story from Jem.

"The first time he did that to me," she told Dan, "I thought sure he had a terrible disease. That reflux thing or some such. Turns out Cody used to do it, too. Sorry you had to get nailed. I should've warned you.''

Dan smiled ruefully. ''Know better next time.'' He nodded at Jem, saying, ''Caught her finger.'' He made it sound like a confession.

''I heard about that,'' Becca said, glancing at her daughter knowingly. ''What I haven't heard yet is what she was doing that she wasn't supposed to be when it happened.''

Jemmy tucked in her chin. ''Just getting something to eat.''

Becca looked at Dan, eyes laughing. ''Always eating lately. Must be gearing up to grow.'' She looked at Jemmy. ''Next time you ask first.''

''I asked,'' she insisted, skewing her gaze sideways.

Becca laid down her fork. ''But did you ask so Dan could see you?''

''No-o-o.''

''I didn't think so, and see what's come of it?''

Jemmy bowed her head. ''I'm sorry.'' Becca lifted her chin with her hand and instructed her with a look to repeat herself to Dan. ''I'm sorry, Daddy.''

Becca gasped and dropped her hand as if she'd been burned. She shot a look at Dan.

He looked positively stricken. ''If I could hear,'' he said softly, ''wouldn't have happened.''

If he could hear, Becca thought to herself, she'd be digging a hole to disappear into right now. It wasn't the first time Dan had failed to pick up on something, and she couldn't say she was sorry. She glared at Jemmy, kept her head turned and whispered fiercely, "Don't you say that again, young lady."

Jemmy folded her arms mutinously. Quickly Becca turned to Dan, engaging him more to keep his attention diverted from Jem than anything else.

"This isn't about you," she said crisply. "It's about her strange notions."

At that Jemmy leaned sideways and hissed, "I don't want a dead daddy no more."

Becca sat frozen for a full five seconds. Time itself seemed to stand still. Finally she turned slightly and took her daughter's face in her hands. "It's not fair, Jem," she said softly. "You can't just pick a daddy and claim him." Jem wrenched her eyes around to look at Dan out of their corners, such longing there that Becca could have wept. "He's been good to us. We'd be bad friends to press him for more, honey."

Jem gulped and nodded. Becca released her, and both subsided into their chairs. After a deep breath, Becca faced Dan once more. His brow was wrinkled with confusion. She cleared her throat and said, "It's got nothing to do with your lack of hearing. She'd have found some way around the rules, wouldn't you, Jem?"

Jemmy looked at Dan with big hangdog eyes and

softly confessed, "I'd of asked real soft 'stead of a-hind your back."

Dan grinned. "That's honest. Apology accepted. Sorry about your finger."

"That's okay," she piped up, staring at her fingertip. "I like it." She held it up for all to see and announced, "I'm polka-dotted!"

Everyone laughed, and the atmosphere lightened a bit. Becca changed the subject to Jessica Schumacher. Jessie could give them only mornings because she'd taken a part-time job helping the school librarian move and reorganize the high school library in order to make room for an array of computers.

"We can manage with that," Dan said.

"Are you sure? I really don't—"

"Want to take advantage," he finished for her. He looked at the kids and smiled. "We'll be fine."

"I'm going to ask around for permanent help," she promised. "Somebody will turn up. They always do."

"Somebody has," he told her quietly, and bent his head over his meal, effectively putting an end to the discussion.

Chapter Fourteen

John Odem showed up just after lunch the next day. Dan was clearing up the dishes, and he turned around to find John in the doorway. He almost started, but he'd turned around so many times lately to find Jem shadowing him that he was beginning to get used to finding himself with company.

"Got anything cold to drink?" John asked, grinning ear to ear.

Dan nodded toward the refrigerator and reached up to pull down a tumbler from a cabinet. "Ice tea."

John took the glass and helped himself. After taking a long swallow, he topped off the glass and turned back to Dan. "Real sweet, just like I like it."

"Jem, too."

"Where do you think she got it from?"

Dan chuckled. "What's up?"

"Nothing. It's my break. Every day but Tuesday and Thursday I work a split shift—four or five hours after opening, four or five hours in the evening to close. I usually go pick up the kids and take them home with me till Becca comes, then I go back to the store. Figured I'd just hang out with you today instead."

Dan blinked at that, but John didn't notice; he'd turned toward the hallway. Bemused, Dan followed him toward the living room. When John reached the center of the hall he winced and looked back over his shoulder. "When you gonna fix that screech?"

"Screen?"

"Scree-*ch*."

"Oh. The squeak."

John pointed at the floor. "That's no piddly squeak, son. That's a banshee in your floor."

"Soon," he said, figuring he'd better get to it quickly before something significant gave way.

John nodded and continued into the living room. He switched on the television before taking the armchair, making himself right to home. Dan figuratively shook his head. Looked as if he had company.

Life had sure changed. Not so long ago, his was the only face he saw in an average day, and only then for as long as it took him to clean up. He'd forgotten what it was like to have people in his life on a routine basis, friends dropping by, others to consider before he started some project or took himself off to bed. It was more complicated this way, but it was also richer.

"Where's the kids?" John asked when Dan looked back to him.

Dan glanced at the monitors clipped to his belt. "CJ's sleeping. Jemmy's out back. Checking on her now." With that he left the room, retracing his steps. When he reached the center of the hall he stopped to feel the give in the floor. Better get under there as soon as possible. If John was going to be around for a while, and it appeared he was, maybe he could slip under there today to take a look.

He went out to find Jem playing with her turtle. He had a hard time figuring out how she could get such enjoyment from a creature with so little personality. Maybe it had something to do with the fact that it paid her no mind and couldn't speed off, since she seemed to jabber nonstop to it as she constantly changed the direction in which it plodded. She was looking forward to the rabbit he'd promised, and they'd built a hutch this morning, but he'd had no opportunity to go shopping. Thankfully, she seemed content with the possibility of getting one for now, and he figured it was a possibility so long as her mama didn't catch wind of their scheme too soon.

"Jem," he called, and she looked up with a smile that squeezed his heart. "Your grandpa's here." He watched her get up off the grass and run to put the turtle back in its pen.

"Do we have to go, Danny?" she asked as she ran up to him.

There it was again. Her pet name for him. He smiled and smoothed a hand down the back of her pale head. "Naw, thought you'd like to know he came for a visit."

"Oh, goody," she said, slipping her hand into his.

They turned and walked back to the house, where she crawled up into her grandfather's lap and settled down to watch a game show. This was how it should be, Dan thought. Becca had to see that eventually. God had shown him; He would show her.

"John," he asked, clearing his throat, "do you mind watching the kids awhile? Want to check under the house about that squeak."

"Sure, son, you go ahead," John said, tilting back his head. "Better you than me."

Dan handed over CJ's monitor and went to change, being careful not to wake the napping boy. Looking in briefly, he found the babe sleeping on his stomach, two fingers in his mouth and his rump sticking in the air. Things had gone easier for them all today, thankfully. He went quietly down the stairs, along the hall and through the kitchen, snatching a flashlight from the utility room as he headed out the back door.

The foundation skirt opened in the back right

next to the water spigot. Dan removed the portable section and set it aside before going down on all fours. He could understand why this sort of thing unnerved some people, but he'd done his share of tunneling and working in close quarters during his time in the Corps. This was nothing compared to some of the work he'd done setting up demolitions and ferreting out explosives. Oddly, that experience served him well now that he'd turned his efforts to building. Funny how life turned out sometimes.

When he'd been whole, he'd taken some extreme chances, often volunteering for the most dangerous jobs. Many times he'd remarked that it was the element of danger that made what he did exciting. Now he was thrilled to stand and watch a little girl talking to a turtle. He took pride in making a lunch she'd eat on the first try and keeping her baby brother happy. Just this morning he'd coaxed CJ up into an independent standing position. Soon the little fellow would take his first steps, and Dan wanted to be there to see it, right alongside his mother.

That was something else he figured he'd better take care of soon, though when he thought of it, his heart pounded as it never had when he'd put his life on the line. Flopping down on his belly and crawling into the dark unknown seemed like a piece of cake in comparison.

Becca looked at Jessica with pure horror. "How long?"

"Five hours," Jessica told her. "When I got here

this morning, he had him a kind of little sled thing with tools and a bag of cement on it all ready to go. Said something about a squeak in the floor.''

Becca knew all about that squeak in the floor. Dan had explained at dinner last evening that a wood support pier had dried out and shrunk, leaving the floor joist to sag. It hadn't cracked yet, but soon would if he didn't get it shored up. When he'd tried to wedge a block of wood in there, however, the beam had started to crumble, so he would have to dig and pour a cement footing for something called a jack pier. She couldn't see how anyone could dig a hole and pour cement under a house without tearing up the floor first, but he'd just shrugged and said there were ways. He'd spoken briefly then about a time when he and his team had actually tunneled beneath a building with their hands under cover of darkness and in dead silence. He hadn't said what for, and she wasn't sure she even wanted to know, but she'd pointed out then that he hadn't been working alone.

''And he knew you had to leave before noon?'' she asked Jessica.

''He said if I'd fix the kids' lunch, he'd come in at eleven forty-five and feed it to them.''

''But he didn't come in.'' Becca bit her lip worriedly.

''And I've just got to go,'' Jessie said, handing over CJ. ''I'm sorry to bring the kids to the store like this. I was supposed to be at the school by one, and I did try to get his attention with a flashlight first. Didn't do any good to holler for him.''

''Dear heaven,'' Becca said, wondering if he was hurt and trapped under there.

Jessie gave Becca a mildly censorial look and said, ''You really ought to get a phone in your house.'' She made a face and added, ''Everybody but me has a cell phone.''

''I don't,'' Becca muttered, spreading her feet to balance CJ's weight on her hip. She was much too worried about Dan at the moment to really think of anything else, let alone correct Jessie's assumption that Dan's house was any part hers or that she and the kids would be there long enough to warrant putting in a phone. ''Thank you, Jessie, and I'm sorry about this.''

As the girl hurried away, Becca turned and called for Abby. Jem had already run back to the deli counter to filch a taste of something from her grandpa. Abby appeared, an anxious look on her face at the sound of Becca's voice.

''Could you watch CJ for a minute? I need to go check on Dan.''

''What on earth?'' Abby began, taking her grandson into her arms.

''He's been under the house for hours, and he knew that Jessica had to leave by noon.''

''You don't think he's been hurt or passed out under there?''

"I just don't know. It's awful hot out. What if he's got heat stroke?"

"Take the car," Abby said. "And maybe you ought to take John, too, just in case."

Becca shook her head, already hurrying away. John would be next to useless in this kind of situation, and Abby couldn't handle the store and the kids on her own. She'd find out what had happened, and if necessary go next door and phone for emergency assistance.

After parking the sedan behind his truck, she rushed around back to find the gaping hole in the foundation skirt. A water hose ran from the spigot outside under the house, its tautness telling her that it had been employed for some purpose. Going down on her hands and knees, she called out to him, even knowing that he couldn't hear her. Peering into the dark, she saw nothing. Could he have gone into the house?

Quickly she shimmied backward and pushed up to her feet. Then she ran across the covered patio and into the house, through the laundry room and the kitchen. The hall was empty, too. For the sake of thoroughness she continued across the hallway into the formal dining room, which was seldom used though the pocket doors between it and the living room were routinely left open. No Dan. She ran for the entry, stuck her head into the study and then climbed the stairs as fast as she could go. She swung into the master bedroom and right on into the bath through the open door. No one.

Back out into the hall she went and through the remaining bedrooms and the second bath. Where could he be? The apartment.

Dashing down the stairs and out the back of the house, she ran for the garage, praying aloud, ''Oh, God, oh, God, please let him be okay. Oh, please. Oh, please.''

Her leg muscles burned with the effort of racing up those steep steps, but she didn't slow until she came to the door. Wrenching the knob, she thrust the door open and literally leaped into the living area. A glance showed her nothing to alleviate her fears. The bedroom and bath proved similarly unhelpful. She was almost sobbing as she ran out again, leaving the door open behind her. She pounded down the stairs, across the drive and through the yard, hitting the ground on knees and palms in front of the foundation opening.

It occurred to her that she should've located the flashlight that Jessie had used, but she wasn't going to waste any more time looking for it. Instead, she dropped to her belly and dug her elbows into the soft dirt just inside the opening, pulling her body forward and into the dark. Blinded by the sudden shift from bright sunlight to inky darkness, she couldn't see a thing.

Craning her neck, she butted her head against a floor joist, driving her teeth together with jaw-cracking force. She ducked down and crawled on, gradually becoming aware that it was cooler here than outside in the sunshine. She heard a rustle of movement, and the word *snake* instantly popped into her head.

Galvanized, she picked up the pace, heedless of her now raw and aching elbows. She didn't bother calling out, knowing that it was wiser to save her energy for what might await ahead. A flashlight suddenly blinked on.

"Becca?"

The light swung around. No longer blinded, she recognized shapes in the gloom: a board on runners stacked with tools, a small shovel and round plastic tub, a large, thick paper bag empty of its contents, levels, rubber mallet, hammer, long, heavy rubber gloves. She saw, too, a scattering of chat or gravel and a number of miscellaneous bits of lumber. In the midst of it sprawled Dan's long, muscular body, one arm flung out, chest gently rising and falling. At least he was alive. Thank God.

"Where are you hurt?"

"What?"

"Where. Are. You. Hurt?"

He flopped over onto his belly and skewed around. "I'm not. Just resting. What's going on?"

Relief flooded her. *Thank You, God.* She touched his face with her hand, somehow needing that physical connection to finally put her fears to rest. Sweet heaven, what would she do if anything ever happened to him? She thought of Cody and what it had meant to lose him, and the horror of also losing Dan brought hot tears to her eyes. Anger quickly followed. "What do you mean, you're not? You've scared the life out of me!"

"Scared?"

"You were supposed to relieve Jessica at eleven forty-five!"

He shoved his wrist into the light beam, checking the time on his watch. "Oh, man."

They stared at each other for a long moment, the flashlight between them. He'd been working and lost track of time. That's all it was. She was ashamed to say that she'd panicked and assumed the worst, but all she'd been able to think at the time was that she might have lost him, too. How she could lose something that wasn't even hers she didn't know.

Finally he said, "Let's get out of here. Go on."

She turned, with some difficulty, and began crawling for the opening. Her muscles felt weak and depleted. Dan pulled ahead, taking the flashlight with him, and got through the opening first. When she finally pushed her upper body out into the sunlight, he reached down and hauled her to her feet. She came to rest against his chest and he held her there, his strong, capable hands clamped around her arms just above the elbows.

"Sorry, honey. Time stands still in dark and silence."

She dropped her gaze. "We thought you'd gotten hurt under there."

"Just busy. Lost track of time."

"You're telling me! It's going on two." Okay, it was almost half past one. In *principle* it was nearly two, which didn't begin to explain why the sap was grinning at her.

"You came to rescue me," he said, linking his hands in the small of her back.

Suddenly she realized how close they were standing, their bodies actually touching, and her heart thumped pronouncedly. She attempted to step back, grumbling, "I came to read you the riot act."

He just grinned and pulled her against him again. Lifting his hands to her face, he slipped his fingers into her hair.

"You came to rescue me."

He bent his head, and somehow she was on her tiptoes, so that their mouths met and melded into sweetness. Cupping her head, he tilted it. Love poured out of her, an endless supply, too long pent up and yearning for expression. Finally he pressed his forehead to hers.

"Don't close up tonight, do you?"

"No."

He lifted his head and let his hands fall away. "Home about six?"

"Yes."

"Where are the kids?"

"At the store."

"Send them back with John."

"All right." She backed away, feeling slightly dazed and disoriented.

"Better change," he said meaningfully, and she looked down at herself.

"Mercy!" Well, what had she expected after dragging herself through the dirt? "Just look at me!"

He lifted his gaze to hers and said loudly, "You're beautiful."

She couldn't help laughing, even as her heart flopped over inside her chest. "I am?"

He just smiled.

It spread through her then—a rare, wonderful knowledge. Everything had changed. The world had fixed itself somehow, as if God had smiled and pronounced creation perfect. All of her worries, all of her fears—some of them unnamed and so unacknowledged until just now—all of her confusion was swept aside in the space between one breath and the next. She didn't know how or why yet. In fact, she had no answers at all at the moment. Yet everything was right, just fine, exactly as it should be.

"I'll get cleaned up," Dan said, moving toward the apartment.

She stood there like a complete idiot, caught in some heavenly snare, until he disappeared across the drive. Turning suddenly, she hurried into the house to do the same.

* * *

"So'd you get finished?"

Dan shook his head at John Odem and explained. "Concrete has to cure. Then put in a pier jack."

John shuddered. "Don't know how you do it. Don't even want to know."

Dan shrugged. "Used to it."

"When you gonna finish Claude Benton's roof?"

"Tomorrow, hopefully."

"I told him you'd get to it soon as you could when he came into the store today. He said not to worry. Want me to let him know you'll be there in the morning?"

"Yes, thanks." He shifted his weight from one foot to the other. "About the kids…"

"What about 'em?"

Dan lifted a hand to the back of his neck. "Could you stay with them till I get back?"

John nodded. "Sure. Where you going?"

"Duncan. Important. Be quick as I can."

John Odem dangled his hands at the ends of his arms, as if shaking the feeling back into them, and said, "I reckon we can manage something."

Dan took a deep breath. "Thing is, don't really want 'em here when Becca gets home."

John's eyebrows went straight up. "Care to tell me why?"

Dan looked him in the eye. "Question to ask. In private."

John's eyebrows climbed higher. "About time, I'd say. Dixon's at the store now, talking to Becca. He wants to bring a fellow out to look at the property, says he's going to build a feedlot."

"That so?" John nodded sagely, and Dan asked, "How do you feel about it?"

"Her selling the place?" John shrugged, his gaze skittering away from Dan's. "That's her business."

"Cody's land," Dan pointed out gently.

John Odem sighed. "Keeping it won't change anything. She could use the money for college funds for the kids. I reckon Cody would want Frank to have it." But it was the end of Cody's dream, and they both knew it. John clapped a hand on Dan's shoulder. "It's as it should be. I wouldn't change it if I could, and that's the truth. No father could take heaven from his son, and I can't say God hasn't provided what we've been missing."

Dan had to look down to hide the sudden sheen in his eyes. "Thanks, John."

John pounded his shoulder. "Welcome to the family, Dan."

"Not yet," Dan pointed out, smiling.

"You will be," John assured him. "I knew soon as she started stopping by Mrs. Buckner's."

"Buckner? The one who taught fifth grade?"

"Same," John acknowledged with a nod of his head.

Dan cocked his, puzzled. "Must be a hundred

years old.'' Why would Becca be seeing old Mrs. Buckner? he wondered.

''She's only eighty,'' John replied, ''and still sharp as a tack.'' Then he waved a hand and asked, ''Got any of that sweet tea?''

Dan chuckled. ''Help yourself.''

''Think I will,'' John said, moving toward the cabinet. He took down a glass, then turned to grin at Dan and said, ''Flowers wouldn't go amiss.''

Dan smiled his thanks for the advice, wishing that his stomach hadn't just turned to cold jelly. ''See what I can do.''

Chapter Fifteen

Fearing he would be short for time, Dan dug out his darkest jeans and pressed them to a military crispness, along with a blue short-sleeved sport shirt that his mother swore was the very color of his eyes. Then he shaved and dressed, buffing his best tooled leather cowboy boots to a shine. He threaded the matching belt through the loops of his jeans, put on his good watch and faced himself in the mirror.

You're deaf, he told himself mentally, as he had so many times before. It had started as a necessary reminder of how his life had changed and gradually had become a test of sorts. Today it felt more like a simple statement of fact, and for the first time it was not followed by a pang of regret but by a brand-new reality check. *You're in love.*

He would not even think about whether or not

the sentiment was mutual. He'd find out soon enough. It was possible, he discovered, to feel elation and terror all at once.

Quickly he descended the stairs, kissed the kids, told them he'd see them later, dropped a grateful hand on John Odem's shoulder and went out to the truck. He fought the urge to speed all the way to Duncan.

Becca slipped through the front door and stopped. The house felt utterly empty. Wherever John Odem had gone with the kids, it wasn't here. She shook her head, feeling hot and irritated. This had been the weirdest day. First Jessica had shown up at the store with the kids, igniting in her an unreasoning terror that had resulted in a belly crawl through the dirt under the house and a toe-curling kiss that she could not even think about for fear of making more of it than was truly there. Then John Odem had shown up at the store with the kids and disappeared again just as she was ready to get off work. She had no idea where they'd gone or what mysterious errand had been important enough for Dan to alter their plans for the day—or where he was now, for that matter.

Painfully aware that she had already overreacted once that day, she was determined not to let her imagination carry her away, but she couldn't help feeling a niggling concern that bordered on annoyance. Surely Abby knew where John had taken the kids, though she'd feigned ignorance, shrugging and telling Becca to head on home.

"We'll get them back to you before bedtime," she'd said, and Becca wondered why even then she'd felt suspicious about that. Jemmy and CJ were undoubtedly safe with their grandfather. Telling herself that she just wasn't used to having any time on her own, she resolutely closed the door, left her small handbag at the foot of the stairs and wandered into the kitchen for something cold to drink.

She pondered whether or not to start dinner and decided to wait, though her stomach rumbled in protest, until she had some idea how many she'd be feeding. Peevishly she wondered if everyone else would eat without thought of her and leave her sitting here alone, starving, all evening. She grabbed a carrot and munched it while she poured a glass of tea, which she carried into the living room.

Stepping out of her shoes, she curled up in the armchair and used the remote to turn on the television, flipping through the channels. Dan had satellite here, so something was always on, but she'd never really developed the TV habit and had no idea what might hold her interest. She settled on a familiar syndicated program from her childhood, but before she could really get into it, she heard Dan's footsteps in the kitchen, accompanied by the faint rustle of paper and plastic. Sliding to the edge of her seat, she prepared to rise, but Dan appeared in the dining room just then, rubbing his hands together.

"Hi. Getting some quiet time?"

She twisted on the seat so that he could see her face. "Yeah. Do you know where John and the kids are?"

"Not a clue. Hungry?"

"Starving." She started to get up again, but he waved her back down.

"Stay there. I brought in Italian. That okay?"

She tilted her head in curiosity. "Where did you get Italian food?"

"Duncan. Watch your program. Won't be a minute." With that, he stepped back and pulled the pocket doors shut.

Becca stared at those closed doors for a moment, decided that he felt he had to make up for scaring her that morning and gingerly sat back. That niggling feeling that all was not as it seemed deepened, however. She endured two more minutes of recorded laugh track before deciding that enough was enough. Aiming the remote control, she shut down the system and rose determinedly to her feet. Striding across the room, she reached for the twin doors, then paused long enough to listen for a moment before sliding them apart.

The table had been set with summer-green place mats and napkins. A small wire basket at one end of the dark, ornate table contained soft, steaming bread sticks. Dan carried two glass goblets into the room and placed them on the table before pulling out a chair for her.

"Sit."

"What's going on?" she asked suspiciously, slowly moving to position herself.

"Thought we'd eat like adults for once," he answered, moving away.

He quickly returned again bearing two of his grandmother's gold-rimmed floral china plates, which Becca had often admired in their mirrored cabinet against the far wall. Reaching across her shoulder, he set one laden plate before her. The aromas of spicy tomato sauce and tangy salad dressing set her stomach to rumbling in anticipation. He laid down the other plate and disappeared again while she was saying how good the food smelled. Seconds later he walked into the room and skirted the table to his own place. Becca's eyes widened at the sight of the vase of hybrid roses in his hands, creamy yellow buds, the color graduating to vibrant pink at the tips of the curling petals.

"These remind me of two favorite women." He pulled out his chair and sat down, saying, "Grandma loved yellow roses. Mom's favorites are hot pink. Makes these special."

"They're beautiful," Becca said. Then she looked him in the eye. "Are we celebrating?"

He shrugged. "Why not?" He reached across the table for her hand. "Mind if I pray?"

"Of course not."

He bowed his head, speaking slowly and deliberately. "Father, thank You for the reminder that this world contains as much beauty as difficulty. Troubles bring us wisdom, so thank You for them, too. My ears don't hear sound, but my heart does. Thank You for this food and this woman. Amen."

He let go of her hand and picked up his fork. Truly moved, Becca stared at him until he glanced up and smiled. He lifted a piece of rotini to his mouth and hummed approval. Once again that feeling that all was utterly right with her world washed over her. What difference did it make what John Odem was up to? Her children were safe with their doting grandpa. Dan had brought her a lovely dinner. Roses adorned the table, and she was now convinced that Frank Dixon truly wanted her property in order to build a feedlot, which would in turn bring a few much-needed jobs to the area and take care of her financial worries. She looked to her plate and picked up her own fork.

They ate in comfortable silence interrupted only by her own voice saying, "This is very good. Thank you."

He just nodded, smiled and went on eating. Finishing way ahead of her, he lounged in his chair, one arm draped over the back, until she finally pushed away her plate.

"I am stuffed," she exclaimed, confessing, "I always eat too much when I'm really hungry."

He swept his gaze over her. "Doesn't show. In fact, you ought to have dessert."

She shook her head. "Thanks, but I really shouldn't."

"Doesn't take up much room," he insisted, rising to his feet. "Italian ice." She rose, too, and began clearing the table, but he took the plates from her hands. "No, no. My shindig."

"Dan," she said, "you don't have to do this. I'm the one who overreacted this morning. It wasn't your fault. You were working hard, and the time just got away from you."

"True. Now sit." He used his elbow on the top of her shoulder to urge her back down into her seat. "Be right back."

She slowly lowered herself onto the chair seat. Something was up, but she couldn't imagine what. Looking at those beautiful roses in that elegant vase, she felt a spark of hope kindle inside her, but she quickly squelched it, afraid to let her imagination run amok. Dan swept back into the room then with a single-footed ice cream bowl of heavy cut glass. He set it in front of her with a flourish, then instead of returning to his place, he dropped down onto the seat of the chair at the end of the table. Were they to share? Becca wondered, looking at the small, ornate bowl. She tilted her head, confused by the yellow-and-pink petals in her bowl.

"These are rose petals."

"Ice underneath."

She fought the impulse to lift a hand to his brow to test it for fever. "What're you doing?"

"Trust me," he said, handing her a spoon. "Go on."

Her heart began to race as she carefully, delicately brushed back the velvety petals with the tip of the spoon until the light caught something in the bottom of the bowl—not ice but gold.

"Oh, no."

The spoon clattered to the table, and with trembling fingers she divided the petals and pushed them apart. Two rows of tiny gold beads formed the band, widening in the middle to create a setting for a large, square-cut stone. Simple, elegant, unique. Definitely an engagement ring—with a very large diamond. She clapped her hands to her cheeks.

"Oh, no!"

She immediately turned to Dan, aware that he was frowning but not quite registering that fact. She was too busy dealing with a host of others. One, from sheer habit and long practice, naturally rose to the fore.

"Please tell me that's not a real diamond!"

"Think I'd give you a fake?" he asked incredulously.

She clapped her hands to her cheeks again. "Oh, no!"

"You don't like it."

"It's beautiful! But you can't—"

Suddenly he sat forward, circled her wrists with his long, strong fingers and tugged her hands away from her face. "Becca, I can be a good husband and father."

"I know that. That's not the point."

"What is?"

"It's too big!"

"What?"

"It costs too much money!" she shouted.

He shook his head as if he hadn't understood a word, and released her. "What does?"

She poked a finger at the crystal bowl, on the verge of tears. "A diamond like that!"

His mouth fell open, and he rolled his eyes. "You won't marry me because the diamond's too big?"

"No! Yes! I mean…" Oh, what was wrong with her? She shook her head. This was not the important part. The important part was "Why?"

"Why?" he echoed uncertainly. "Why do I want to marry you?"

A tear sneaked out of the corner of her eye. She reached up a hand to deal with it, saying very clearly, "You're a natural-born hero, Daniel Holden, but you can't rescue the whole world."

"Not trying to." He caught her hands again and pressed them together, palm to palm, with his own. "Becca," he said earnestly, "God took my hearing to get me here to you."

Her chin began to wobble. "To rescue us from the storm, you mean?"

"To rescue *me*." He clasped his hands around hers. "I was so busy I couldn't hear God saying I wasn't doing what He wanted. He had to make me *really* listen. Understand?"

She had to ponder it a moment, but then she nodded. "I think so." Pulling her hands away, she wiped both cheeks. "But that doesn't mean you're supposed to marry me."

"Becca," he said, "I can't imagine my life without you and the kids. I don't want to."

The sobs caught her by surprise, and she wasn't sure what they came from—relief, joy, stubborn fear. Maybe all of it. Her heart felt so full suddenly that it seemed about to burst. The look of dismay on Dan's face just made her cry all the harder.

"Don't. Please, Becca, be happy. Forget everything else. I just want you to be happy. You deserve it. Sweetest, dearest, most beautiful woman on earth."

She laughed and sobbed and found herself horribly mute when she most wanted, needed to tell him what she was feeling. Suddenly she knew just how to do it. Her hands stumbled through the gestures. Once, twice. The third time he slipped off his chair onto his knees and wrapped his arms around her.

"I know," he said. "I love you, too. Love you so much."

She laughed and sniffed and laughed until he pulled back, smoothing her hair away from her face with his big, warm, protective hands. "Where did you learn?"

She tried to tell him, but her voice broke. She spelled it out with her fingers. B-u-c-k-n-e-r.

He smiled. "So that's what that was about."

She nodded and gasped and held on to him by his shirt, her hands grasping the fabric at his sides. He sat back on his heels and quickly signed something. All she got was "you" and "me."

"I'm not very good yet," she told him. "You have to say it."

He went more slowly this time, speaking as he signed. "Will you marry me?"

She covered her trembling mouth with one hand and nodded decisively. Beaming, he reached into the bowl and scooped out the ring, which he then slid onto her finger, saying, "Don't like it, we'll exchange it."

"I love it, but can we afford it?" she asked anxiously.

Dan chuckled and got to his feet, pulling her up and clasping his hands in the small of her back. "Not rich, but well fixed. I can give us a good life, Becca."

She bit her lip and looked at the ring, her hand resting lightly against his chest. "Come to think of it, I'm going to have some money, too. Frank's serious about the feedlot, you know."

"There you go. All that worry, you don't even need rescuing."

She blinked at him in shock. "That's right!" Why hadn't she realized it before? God had taken care of everything, as always, even her own stupid fears. "I've been an awful fool," she managed to say, glad he couldn't hear the screeching whine of her voice.

"No. No, no. Crisis confuses everything. I was confused, too, for long time." He smiled wryly. "Then this morning *you* came to rescue *me*, and I finally heard."

Her pulse quickened. "What did you hear?"

He cupped her face in his hands and smiled down into her eyes. "Your heart speaking to mine."

She slid her arms around his neck and laid her head on his shoulder, feeling the warmth and strength and rightness of his embrace. "I'll marry you, Dan Holden," she whispered, "and thank God every day for you." She knew that he heard, just not with his ears.

"A real wedding," Dan insisted later, sitting on the sofa next to her, his arms looped about her shoulders. He couldn't stop grinning, couldn't stop marveling, couldn't stop touching her, loving her. He smiled as she considered, watching the cogs turning in her mind. Sweet Becca, she just couldn't seem to stop counting pennies, but then she did.

"I'd like that, too. I didn't have it with Cody,

didn't think it was important, and even if I had, my folks couldn't have provided cupcakes, let alone wedding cake. Besides, he had to be in Calgary in two days. I'd like a church wedding this time, the last time.''

The last time. Dan liked that.

''Nothing fancy,'' he said, ''but with my folks and yours, if they'll come.'' He felt strong, certain. Whole. Funny how that had nothing at all to do with physical perfection.

''I'm not sure they will,'' Becca was saying, ''but we'll invite them.''

''Okay. When?''

She shrugged. ''As soon as we can work it out. I want to talk to Abby and John. And Jemmy.''

He nodded. ''Better see how the kids take to it first, huh?''

Becca cut him a look. ''Oh, they'll 'take to it,' all right. Trust me on that.''

''CJ's little,'' Dan mused. ''Don't figure he'll mind. Jem might be little confused, but she'll be okay eventually.''

''Eventually,'' Becca echoed. It almost seemed like a question. She shifted around on the couch to face him more fully, drawing up one leg. ''You don't read lips as well as you think you do, hotshot.''

He frowned, targeting his concentration. ''How's that?''

Her lips twitched. "Jemmy decided some time ago that you are her father."

"What?" He couldn't have gotten that right.

"You think she's been calling you Danny, don't you?"

His brows drew together. She *had* been calling him Danny. Unless... His eyes widened. "Daddy?"

"Yep." His jaw dropped, and Becca just grinned. "We've been around and around about it, but she's one stubborn little girl."

"Daddy," Dan whispered. He'd thought he'd never be anyone's daddy, and then he was without even realizing it. He had to duck his head, the tears catching him unawares. Becca slipped her hand into his, and he heard it again.

"I love you. Just as you are."

He got to his feet, pulling her up with him. "Let's go."

He wanted to hear Jem call him "Daddy" and John Odem call him "son" and Becca tell them all that she loved him and trusted him enough to be his bride. He wanted to hear Abby's delight and CJ's sweet confusion and silly bids for attention. He could already hear Cody whispering that he should take care of them, make them his own.

The sound of a heart speaking was a beautiful thing.

*   *   *   *   *

Dear Reader,

Hearing impairment is a serious issue in my family. In 1996 my beautiful niece Hillary gave birth under very trying circumstances that even involved airlifting her newborn daughter a hundred miles away to a special hospital. After fearing that our Madison wouldn't survive or could do so only with extreme medical problems, we thanked God to find that her sole impairment was loss of hearing. What a blessing she's been to us!

Her parents have always treated Madi as the perfectly normal child she is, so our darling not only speaks normally, reads on grade level, enjoys television and, yes, even music, she's also made significant accomplishments in her young life that few hearing children have achieved. Last year, her parents allowed her to enroll in competitive cheerleading, and her team went on to win two national championships in the mini-tot division. Madison herself won the American's Elite National Championship for Individual Dance at the age of six in Kansas City, Kansas. A world champion at six! How's that for inspiration?

As Madi could tell you, love, strong support, hard work and prayer can overcome any personal challenge, which is Dan Holden's message for us in this book. Like Dan, Madi knows she's "challenged," and that's sometimes daunting, but—also like Dan—our little rosebud has bloomed huge under the bright light of personal accomplishment. I hope you enjoy their story. And look out, world, here comes Madison Bowles! (Go get 'em, baby.)

God Bless,

Arlene James

Love Inspired®

AUTUMN PROMISES

BY

KATE WELSH

Evan Alton had cut himself off from most of the
world, except his children, for years. But when his
twin grandbabies needed him, the rancher would do
anything, even allow the infuriating Meg Taggert to
stay on the ranch to help. Yet caring for the twins
brought him and Meg close, and made Evan feel
alive for the first time in years. Perhaps the babies
weren't the only ones Meg was sent to help....

Don't miss

AUTUMN PROMISES

On sale August 2004

Available at your favorite retail outlet.

Love Inspired®

LOVE ENOUGH FOR TWO

BY

CYNTHIA RUTLEDGE

Single mom Sierra Summers worked hard to create a loving, stable home for her daughter. Men were not part of the equation—until attorney Matthew Dixon walked into her store with a proposition that threatened her resolve. Neither Sierra nor Matt were thinking marriage, but maybe God had a different path for them....

Don't miss

LOVE ENOUGH FOR TWO

On sale August 2004

Available at your favorite retail outlet.

Take 2 inspirational love stories FREE!

PLUS get a FREE surprise gift!

Mail to Steeple Hill Reader Service™

In U.S.	In Canada
3010 Walden Ave.	P.O. Box 609
P.O. Box 1867	Fort Erie, Ontario
Buffalo, NY 14240-1867	L2A 5X3

YES! Please send me 2 free Love Inspired® novels and my free surprise gift. After receiving them, if I don't wish to receive anymore, I can return the shipping statement marked cancel. If I don't cancel, I will receive 4 brand-new novels every month, before they're available in stores! Bill me at the low price of $4.24 each in the U.S. and $4.74 each in Canada, plus 25¢ shipping and handling and applicable sales tax, if any*. That's the complete price and a savings of over 10% off the cover prices—quite a bargain! I understand that accepting the books and gift places me under no obligation ever to buy any books. I can always return a shipment and cancel at any time. Even if I never buy another book from Steeple Hill, the 2 free books and the surprise gift are mine to keep forever.

113 IDN DZ9M
313 IDN DZ9N

Name _____ (PLEASE PRINT)

Address _____ Apt. No. _____

City _____ State/Prov. _____ Zip/Postal Code _____

Love Inspired

FINDING AMY

BY

CAROL STEWARD

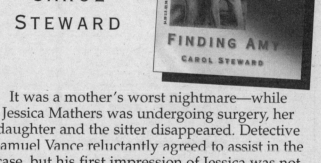

It was a mother's worst nightmare—while Jessica Mathers was undergoing surgery, her daughter and the sitter disappeared. Detective Samuel Vance reluctantly agreed to assist in the case, but his first impression of Jessica was not favorable. Yet Sam quickly learned that Jessica was a warm, caring mother. Could their faith help them find Amy...and forge a relationship?

Don't miss

FINDING AMY

On sale August 2004

Available at your favorite retail outlet.

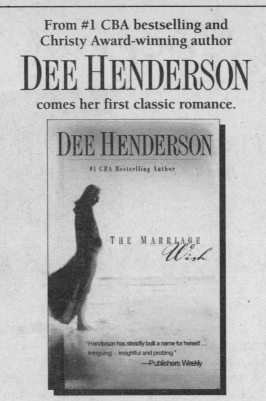